# TROPICAL EDEN

GW00320226

Devon Matthews was dismayed when her father announced he might be selling their island home—especially when she found out who the prospective buyer was. Hunt Kincaid was the most insufferable man she had ever met—so why did she find herself responding to his kisses?

# TROPICAL EDEN

BY
## KERRY ALLYNE

## MILLS & BOON LIMITED
### 15–16 BROOK'S MEWS
### LONDON W1A 1DR

*First published 1984*
*Australian copyright 1984*
*Philippine copyright 1984*
*This edition 1984*

© *Kerry Allyne* 1984

ISBN 0 263 74872 3

*Set in Monophoto Plantin 10 on 11½ pt.*
*01–1284 – 51387*

*Made and printed in Great Britain by*
*Richard Clay (The Chaucer Press) Ltd,*
*Bungay, Suffolk*

# CHAPTER ONE

WITH one hand raised to shade eyes the same colour as
the aquamarine sea she was looking out on from the
verandah of her large, rambling guesthouse home,
Devon Matthews' vision concentrated on the luxury
powered yacht navigating the narrow channel through
the coral that surrounded Cowrie Island. Situated in
the northern section of Australia's Great Barrier Reef,
it was a popular safe anchorage for many privately
owned vessels, but the one now entering the inner
lagoon was obviously of a class that normally preferred
the docking facilities available on the mainland, and
with a slight frown of curiosity marking her forehead
she turned to the deeply tanned, white-haired man
sitting on the steps just beside her, mending a sail.

'That's the same boat that was cruising around here
about a week or so ago, isn't it, Dad?' she mused.

Leaving his labour of love for a moment Granville
Matthews lifted his head in order to cast a searching
gaze across the glinting, dazzling water. 'Mmm, that's
the same one all right,' he nodded as his hazel eyes
came to rest on the gleaming vessel. 'She's a beauty,
isn't she?'

'You certainly won't get any arguments about that,'
Devon half laughed wryly. 'But I wonder why she's
calling in here instead of Northport.' Their nearest
harbour and town on the mainland. 'It's only another
few hours' sailing time away.'

Her father shrugged, his attention returning to the

5

sail spread about him. 'Admittedly, it's not the type of boat we usually have mooring here and camping down with the rest of the yachties, but who knows, maybe they've got a spot of engine trouble they want to attend to, or perhaps they just don't want to go on to Northport today.' He looked up again, his expression humorously quizzical. 'Does it matter? And why the interest, anyway?'

Devon shook her head, wondering much the same herself, her wavy golden hair bouncing about her own smoothly suntanned shoulders that were only covered by thin straps of a clinging lemon sun-top. 'I don't know, just because I didn't expect to see them this way again so soon, or for them to call here, I guess,' she grinned, her widely curving mouth shaping ruefully. 'Anyhow, they'll probably be off again in the morning.' The prediction was accompanied by a dismissive movement of her hands as she began descending the steps on bare feet. 'Meanwhile, I'm off for a swim before I have to help Aunt Violet fix dinner.'

'Garth not going with you?' Her father's brows rose enquiringly.

'No, he's engrossed in some book he wants to finish reading and said he'd give it a miss this afternoon.' Garth Wilkinson was her fiancé from the mainland who was holidaying with them for a month.

Granville Matthews nodded, his wiry, weather-beaten fingers resuming their stitching. 'Well, don't be late, you know we've got a couple more guests than usual at the moment—plus Garth, of course—and Violet needs your help.'

'Don't worry, I won't forget,' she promised with a smile and turned for the rear of the wooden, colonial-styled building where she collected a towel from the washing line before proceeding down the decidedly rocky path that led to her favourite swimming venue.

Coming out from between the shading palms and casuarinas some minutes later, Devon stopped momentarily on the creeper covered dunes above Careen Beach, the view spread before her never failing to impress her with its beauty, despite having seen it so many times before.

Sheltered between two small headlands the area was completely secluded, the white sand sparkling beneath the blazing sun that was beating hotly against her back. Inside the protective reef the waters of the lagoon were an incredibly clear yellow-green, while those washing over the coral were pure azure. Further out the sea changed colour again, this time to a deeper, more intense blue, as the grooves and buttresses of the reef front dropped sharply to the ocean floor below. Towards the horizon the scene was repeated again and again where each successive reef, washed over by white-capped waves rolling in from the Pacific, had formed its own picturesque lagoon within its coral ramparts—to the delight of airborne sightseers and photographers, if not always to sailors, for the very aspects that made them such a sight to behold also created hazardous conditions at sea.

Not that any such troubling thoughts were on Devon's mind as she presently stepped on to the beach and dropped her towel on the coral sand before divesting herself swiftly of her ribbed cotton top and shorts. She never bothered donning a swimming costume when she came here alone, preferring to experience the silky sensation of the water gliding unhindered along her darkly golden length, and

knowing that the rugged track leading down to this
particular beach was an ample deterrent to any of the
rather elderly visitors staying at the guesthouse, and
the high tide meant no one would be reef-walking
around the headland that afternoon either. The
yachtsmen who came ashore and camped on the other
side of the island she had no worries about
whatsoever. They had always respected her father's
request that they remain within the generous area
allotted for their use, unless there was some specific
reason for them to come to the house. It was a
privately owned island, after all.

Now, as she dived cleanly into the warm inviting
water, she swam leisurely for a few strokes, her eyes
automatically seeking any changes brought about by
the changing tides, any new inhabitants that may have
made their way into the lagoon from over the reef or
from somewhere else around the island. Having lived
there for the whole of her twenty-two years, no one
knew the island or its fringing reef better than Devon
did—except perhaps her father—and she never tired
of watching its underwater life forms. The variety was
so great, and in many instances so colourful, that it
often captured her attention for hours. A recollection
that had her abruptly, determinedly, rising to the
surface again and smiling ruefully to herself. If she
wasn't careful she *would* forget all about the time and
that wouldn't exactly put her in her aunt's good graces
at all—as well as being unfair to that very industrious
lady, she owned honestly. So with a regretful grimace
she made do with merely swimming the length of the
lagoon a couple of times, before returning to the beach
to dry off in the sun. Lying back on her towel Devon
pulled her cotton top over her face to provide it with

some protection from the burning rays and closed her eyes, her thoughts lingering on her aunt as her shapely body relaxed in the hot, still atmosphere.

Violet Matthews, Granville's younger, unmarried sister, had resigned from her position as assistant chef at a large hotel on the mainland and had moved on to the island more or less uninvited, though no less appreciated for all that, when her sister-in-law had died as a result of complications setting in after she had given birth to Devon—her first and only child, if one discounted three previous miscarriages—at the rather late age of forty-five. Since that time Violet had made herself indispensable, helping to rear her niece and run the guesthouse.

In those days Cowrie Island had catered to a far greater number of visitors than it did now, for as more and more resorts opened on other islands—and with easier, more comfortable forms of access than the weekly trading launch that serviced Cowrie—the guesthouse's popularity had waned considerably, so that now their guests were mainly in the retired age bracket who had no objections to making their own amusement during their stay. Of course the consequent drop in revenue had been very noticeable but by careful budgeting, supplemented the last few years by the income Devon earned with her designs for T-shirts and other souvenirs that were sold in a tourist shop in Northport, the family had been able to get by, and as none of them was really interested in seeing the island overrun with visitors they considered the financial hardships that did occur from time to time to be well worth it in order to retain their way of life.

With a pleasurable sigh Devon pulled her top from her face, preparing to roll over on to her stomach, but

as she did so her eyes suddenly snapped wide open in
dismay, and indignation, on seeing a tall male figure
standing no more than a few yards away, his deep
blue, assessing gaze totally unabashed in its thorough
scrutiny of *her*! Gasping, she flipped her towel across
her slender, flaring hips and clutched her sun-top to
her chest as she rapidly gained a sitting position.

'Get out of here!' she blazed furiously even as her
cheeks burnt with a mortifying heat at having been so
discovered. 'How dare you come peeping and prying!
This is private property and you've no right being on
this beach!'

Strong, square hands came to rest on lean, shorts-
clad hips above which a navy T-shirt outlined a broad
and powerfully muscled chest. 'I wasn't peeping—just
admiring the scenery. It's quite—umm—spectacular,
isn't it?' the stranger drawled in a drily expressive tone
that brought new waves of embarrassed colour to her
face.

Having expected an apology, at least, Devon's ire
mounted uncontrollably at the thought that he found
both her predicament and her embarrassment amusing—as manifested by the dancing lights he didn't
bother to disguise in the depths of his ebony-lashed eyes.

'It's no different to the scenery on the other side of
the island!' she claimed heatedly, if a little distractedly.
'And that's where you yachties are supposed to stay!
You're not permitted, and *you* especially are not
wanted over here, and if you don't leave immediately
I'll have my father ban you from Cowrie altogether!'
She drew a heaving breath. 'Which boat are you from,
anyway?'

'The *Kanandah*,' he supplied negligently. 'We
arrived this afternoon.'

The luxury one she had watched making its way through the reef. He was probably one of the crew. 'Well, couldn't you read the signs saying this part of the island's off limits? Or did you just think it didn't apply to you because yours is the most expensive vessel there?' Her voice became strongly overlaid with sarcasm.

His firm, sensuously shaped mouth sloped crookedly. 'Not exactly. We were simply told that if we wanted to see Granville Matthews we could find him at the house.'

We! There was someone else with him? Devon spared a hasty, anxious look around but thankfully could see no sign of anyone else. 'Then you don't appear to be a particularly competent navigator because the house is that way!' she retorted on an acid note, pointing back over the dunes. 'It's a large wooden building I wouldn't have believed anyone could miss!'

'Oh, I didn't miss it,' he advised casually. 'I just came on past it in order to have a look around.'

Devon pressed her lips together infuriatedly. The gall of the man when he was aware he was trespassing! 'Then I hope you enjoyed your look, mister, because it's the last one you'll ever get of this island, believe me! When I get through telling my father about this you'll be off of here so fast your feet won't touch the ground!'

Surprisingly, he grinned unconcernedly at that, his teeth shining whitely against the bronze of his skin. 'I doubt it. And as for enjoying my look round . . .' he paused, his glance significant as it roved deliberately over her only partially covered form, 'well, there's certainly no question that I did that.'

Devon grudgingly averted her gaze. It was impossible to appear dignified and in control when one was almost naked, and particularly when a boorish intruder purposely reminded her of the fact.

'Besides . . .' she suddenly realised he was continuing in the same lazily mocking voice, 'it was Granville Matthews—your father, I presume?—who gave his consent for my coming this way.'

'That's a damned lie!' Her wide-spaced and darkly fringed eyes locked fiercely with his again. 'He'd never do such a thing!'

'Because he's aware of your liking for sunbathing in such a—er—natural state?'

'No! He doesn't even know that I. . .' Flushing once more she came to a halt, biting at her lip in annoyance for having been nettled into making even such a fractional disclosure. Knowing her prim and proper aunt would never, never have approved of such behaviour had always kept her silent on the subject. That was, until this unwelcome, insensitive lout had come along! She began again with a disparaging snap, 'No, because he also values our privacy, and because he's got no time either for those who come pushing in here as if they own the place just because they happen to be on the biggest yacht! So as I said, when I tell him. . .'

'That I disturbed his daughter while she was in the altogether?' he inserted tauntingly. 'Or perhaps we could tell him together, hmm? That way he may understand why you're so incensed at my presence.'

'He'll understand anyway!' she glared at him balefully. 'But now, since you've had your look round, you can just clear off! I want to get dressed!'

'So don't let me stop you,' he shrugged indolently,

remaining exactly where he was. 'I've already seen everything there is to see, after all.'

Did he have to keep reminding her! 'As well as all you're going to!' she gritted. 'So you can leave—right now! Or would you prefer it if I started screaming for help?'

'What, and allow whoever comes to see you so charmingly unclothed too?'

She hadn't considered that, and if it should happen to be Garth who arrived she was positive she would never hear the end of it. At times he could be almost as straitlaced as Aunt Violet. 'Then you might at least have the decency to look the other way instead of— instead of. . .'

'Being honest enough to admit appreciating what I see?'

She sucked in a stormy breath. 'Instead of trying to humiliate me for your own amusement, you—you ill- mannered creep!'

Not even that seemed to perturb him, or have him experiencing an attack of consideration. 'I wouldn't precisely call you gracious either, sweetheart,' he merely countered in wry accents.

'Why should I be? *I'm* not the one who's trespassing!'

'And neither am I.'

If she had been in a position to do so, Devon might have thrown something at him. 'Says you! Now are you going to leave or not?'

'And thereby spoil my unmannerly image?' He flexed a wide shoulder, his gaze mocking as it held hers. 'I see no reason why I should.'

No, he probably didn't. His overly assured type always did think they could act as they pleased, regardless of anyone else! But if he didn't intend to depart, just how *was* she going to get dressed without revealing more of herself than was already subject to his openly assessing, aggravating perusal?

With another glare for his insensitivity she swivelled around as best she was able until her back was to him and then proceeded to drag her lemon top over her head with fumbling fingers, cursing inwardly that it should choose this particular time to stick to her heated skin and, as a result, make the exercise that much more difficult and lengthy. Thankfully, however, her shorts and pants were rather more accommodating and by managing to wrap the towel around herself a little more securely she was able to hitch these more or less into place with a few hurried movements.

Feeling decidedly more comfortable now, Devon promptly sprang to her feet, gave her shorts a couple of righting tugs before tossing her towel over one shoulder, and stalked past her audience with her head held high but without saying another word. Actually, she was so furious only physical retribution would have served as a release for her feelings, but as the man—even taller and more solidly built than she had previously thought, she noted on drawing level with him—had already proved to possess no finer instincts, she considered such an action on her part could be just a touch imprudent. There was a distinct possibility he might respond in kind, and having no doubt just who would come off worst from such an encounter she had to be content with picturing her father ordering him off the island for good once she informed him they had a brazen trespasser in their midst.

'If you're going back to the house I'll go with you,' the casual declaration was suddenly made behind her, and had her spinning about wrathfully, her already seething temper threatening to boil over. Oh, yes, he was willing to leave now, wasn't he?

'No, thanks, I'd rather go on my own!' she snubbed between clenched teeth. 'I'm rather particular about who I'm seen with!'

'One wouldn't know it if that patronising excuse for a man up at the house is your fiancé,' he returned with a contemptuous half laugh.

Devon gasped, hardly able to credit his effrontery. 'How dare you!' she exploded. 'What would you know about Garth, anyway? And for your information, there's more to being a man than just muscles and a macho attitude, you know!'

'Sure,' he agreed drily, closing the gap between them leisurely. 'But just being male doesn't necessarily make him one either, beautiful. As for what I know about him. . .' He paused, his lips twisting eloquently. 'I met him . . . that was enough.'

'Oh?' Her winged brows peaked caustically. 'And when would that have been? When he discovered you trespassing and informed you in no uncertain terms that your presence was unwelcome? Is that why you're trying to belittle him now?'

'Uh-uh.' He shook his head as he came to a halt just before her, and making Devon feel her own five foot six height relatively stunted in comparison. She guessed him to be six foot two at least. 'It was while Royce and I were talking to your father. He introduced us.'

For a moment she could only stare at him indecisively as doubts began to creep into her mind for the first time. He sounded so positive that it was becoming more and more difficult to continue gainsaying his contention. The Royce he mentioned she presumed to be the companion he had spoken of earlier.

'And—and why would he do that?' she consequently stammered on a rather less confident note.

'Because he happened to be there at the time, I guess,' he drawled whimsically. His darkly blue eyes filled with lazy goading. 'Although why he would be when his fiancée is disporting herself down here like a free-spirited child of nature, God only knows. I certainly wouldn't be if such a long-limbed and shapely sea nymph wore my ring on her finger.'

'No, I'm sure you wouldn't!' Devon retorted acidly, attempting to ignore the unbidden colour his description had brought to her cheeks. 'You'd have neither the good taste nor the consideration to behave in any other fashion than the offensive one you've already displayed! Just like others of your kind, you're doubtlessly only capable of a "grab and subdue" approach with regard to the opposite sex!'

One corner of his mouth tilted sardonically. 'You mean, like this?' he quizzed, and before she realised what was happening two tanned hands had indeed grabbed hold of her and dragged her disconcertingly close to a hard chest.

Devon's lips parted involuntarily in a mixture of shock and fury, but before she could close them again they were captured determinedly by a mouth she discovered to be incredibly seductive in its skilful exploration of their soft contours, and not forcefully quelling as she had anticipated at all. So persuasive was it, in fact, that she soon found to her horror they were beginning to soften pliantly beneath the tantalising contact, and her breathing was erratic as she belatedly wrested herself free.

'Ex-exactly!' she finally answered his facetious question with as much sarcastic conviction as she could muster. 'You've proved my point!'

'And you mine,' came the impenitent, mocking return.

'Meaning?'

'If your fiancé was really worth his salt, you wouldn't be so receptive to another man's kisses,' he drawled lazily.

Devon crimsoned. 'I was not r-receptive!' she spluttered embarrassedly, defensively. 'I—I was surprised and shocked, that's all. I'm not accustomed to being grabbed and kissed by total strangers!'

'Nor by your fiancé, at a guess,' he proposed on the driest of notes.

'Not in that manner, no, I'm glad to say!' she derived considerable satisfaction from refuting hotly. 'And I'll thank you to keep your unwanted comments concerning Garth to yourself! He's nothing whatever to do with you!' And with a defiant toss of her head she began heading for the track leading up to the house once more, and at a pace she hoped would leave him behind. The man's audacity appeared limitless!

Unfortunately, it was a hope doomed to disappointment because his longer, muscled legs could cover the ground even faster than hers could, leaving her no recourse but to studiously ignore him instead as he followed her up the narrow, uneven path.

'It's a real tropical Eden, isn't it?' he remarked at one stage where the lush vegetation, filled with fan palms, twining vines and flourishing ferns, encroached to within inches of them.

Devon remained silent for a few seconds, but the opportunity was too good to pass and she flicked him a grimacing glance over her shoulder. 'Mmm, complete with snake too, unfortunately, at the moment!' she gibed meaningfully.

His ensuing laugh was amused and as they continued on their way she strangely, annoyingly, found her thoughts waywardly centring about him. She surmised him to be in his early thirties, around thirty-four probably, and with his roughly handsome features and disturbingly flagrant disregard for the proprieties, she didn't doubt he could spell disaster for any female unfortunate enough to arouse his interest.

Not that it wasn't apparent some hapless members of her own sex hadn't already suffered for having done so—just the confident, experienced fashion in which he had kissed herself had demonstrated he was no stranger to success where women were concerned—as well as it being equally obvious he considered all women fair game, whether attached or not. His presumptuous behaviour towards herself when he was fully aware she was already engaged had more than adequately shown that!

While as for his remarks regarding Garth . . . well, so what if he was of a rather more scholarly than active disposition, or that his emotions were a little restrained. At least that was preferable to not bothering to control them at all, wasn't it?

Reaching the end of the track first, Devon hurried across the intervening lawn towards the front verandah of the house where she could see her father seated in a cane chair, deep in conversation with a rather distinguished looking man of some fifty years who was dressed neatly in a pair of fawn slacks and short-sleeved, cream shirt. They made a somewhat incongruous pair, she mused absently as she bounded agilely up the steps, for her parent was still wearing his old, stained working shorts, his weather-beaten chest devoid of any covering at all.

Their conversation ceased and they both rose to their feet at her approach, but with only a faint half smile of acknowledgment for his companion—that he had some connection with the younger man negligently following her made him almost as unwelcome as far as she was concerned—she headed straight for her father.

'Dad, did you give. . .'

'Ah, Devon!' He started speaking at the same time, causing her to break off. 'I'd like you to meet Royce Attwood. He's from the yacht we noticed coming in this afternoon.' And with obvious pride to the pleasant-faced man beside him, 'My daughter, Devon, Royce.'

'How do you do?' she responded cursorily, and a little hastily, to the older man's subsequent greeting, anxious only to return to the question she had been about to ask, but merely to find her father hadn't finished yet.

'I see you've already met Hunter,' he went on with a smile that encompassed the T-shirted man now beside her.

'Regretfully!' she gave vent to her feelings, and accompanied it with an emphasising glare at the subject of her simmering resentment. She also wasn't averse to hoping that if his associate should just happen to have some position of authority aboard the yacht, her annoyance at one of the crew's presence might not go unreported.

'Oh?' Granville Matthews looked from one to the other of them in obvious surprise, and just as obviously at a loss for something to say.

It was left to Royce Attwood to prompt, wryly askance, 'Hunt . . .?'

From his position where he now leant casually against the verandah rail, his arms folded lightly across his broad chest, Hunt gave an indolent shrug. 'It appears I upset the—umm—lady by abruptly interrupting her solitude when she . . .' pausing, it was he who spared Devon a glance this time—a glinting, taunting glance that had her eyes widening in dismay and unconscious pleading at the thought of what he had the power to reveal in retaliation, 'definitely wasn't expecting any company,' he turned back to the others to conclude in dry tones. And to Devon's heartfelt relief!

'Oh, I see,' nodded Granville understandingly, his smile returning. Then, to his daughter curiously, 'Although I must admit I find it hard to understand why that should apparently have annoyed you to quite such a degree.'

'Yes—well . . .' She hunched one shoulder diffidently, and feeling obliged now not to disclose all that had infuriated her in return for her own secret having been kept, 'I—I just couldn't bring myself to believe you'd given someone permission to explore Careen Beach, I suppose. You never have before.' She still couldn't help sounding just a trifle accusing.

'No, but then I didn't expect you to resent it so vigorously this one time either,' he chided gently. 'It wasn't as if I allowed a whole party of people down there when all's said and done.'

It might have been better if he had! And she was still puzzled as to why he had permitted *anyone* to look over the area anyway. In the past he had always insisted on retaining their privacy as much as she had.

'No, but perhaps if I hadn't been quite so unprepared. . .' Her voice trailed away uncomfortably, her awkwardness increasing as she caught sight of Hunt's humorous expression, knowing he was remembering just *how* unprepared she had been. Briefly, a woman appeared at the far end of the verandah to water a couple of hanging baskets of brightly flowering cacti and Devon sighed gratefully for the legitimate excuse it afforded her to escape. 'Oh, there's Aunt Violet,' she exclaimed. 'She's expecting me to help with the dinner so I'm afraid you'll have to excuse me.' She turned more towards the older of their two visitors. 'I don't imagine I'll be seeing you again,' most of the yachtsmen who came to the island usually only stayed a couple of days before moving on, and she couldn't envisage a yacht like the *Kanandah* being any different, 'so I'll. . .'

'Oh, I'm sure you'll be seeing more of them,' interposed her father with a smile. 'They're not really anticipating leaving for a while yet.'

It was all Devon could do not to grimace despairingly at the totally unexpected information. Theirs was a boat she would have been delighted to see depart as soon as possible—along with one especially unwelcome member of its complement! 'I see,' she acknowledged weakly, disappointedly. 'In that case, it appears I may see you again later, after all.' And with a half smile in Royce Attwood's direction she headed for her room and a shower.

Twenty minutes later, and wearing a lime green and black, thin cotton sunfrock this time, Devon arrived in the large kitchen at the back of the house where her aunt, trim and prim as always, had already begun preparing the evening meal.

'I'm sorry if I'm late,' she apologised sincerely as she immediately set about washing some of the salad vegetables they would be requiring and which had already been laid on the sink. 'I got caught up with those men talking to Dad.' Pausing, she sent a frowning look across to the table. 'How come he seems so friendly with them, especially on such short notice? I mean, he even allowed one of them to explore our side of the island, and he's definitely never done anything like that before.'

Momentarily, her aunt stopped what she was doing, her greying brows drawing together thoughtfully. 'No, he certainly hasn't,' she agreed. 'Although I've no doubt he had a good reason for it.' With a slight shrug of her thin shoulders she resumed peeling some carrots. 'He wouldn't give such permission lightly, I'm sure.'

Devon didn't think he would either, and that was what made it all the more enigmatic. 'Mmm, but what reason? And on such short acquaintance too!'

'As to that I couldn't say, dear. I only met them very briefly—I had too much to do in here to stay and talk—but they both seemed very likeable, and very taken with the island, so maybe that's why.'

*Both* likeable? There was no way Devon could endorse that claim! 'We've had others here, though, who would fit that description equally well, but they were never able to prevail upon him to relax the rules,' she pointed out.

Violet bustled across to rinse the carrots in the other bowl of the sink prior to tipping them into a saucepan. 'Yes, well, I think you'll just have to ask your father about that later. Or perhaps Garth knows,' she added as an afterthought. 'He was also talking to them for a while when they first arrived.'

So she had been told, Devon recalled testily, but at least it sounded a little more promising that her fiancé could be able to throw some light on the subject before too much longer. He usually put in an appearance just as they were concluding the dinner preparations, whereas her father normally liked to put in some work on his own small sloop at this time of day and as a result was invariably late for the meal.

'And just where is Garth, by the way?' she quizzed lightly. 'I couldn't see him when I returned from my swim. Don't tell me he's back in his room again doing more reading.' With a partly disbelieving laugh.

'I wouldn't be at all surprised,' said Violet, turning her attention to some broccoli now. 'He rarely seems to do much else while he's here.'

'Oh, I don't know about that,' Devon defended staunchly. 'He climbed to the top of The Pinnacle,' the highest point on the island, 'with me this morning.'

Her aunt gave her an old-fashioned look. 'Then complained all through lunch about how his legs ached in consequence.'

'He's just not used to it, that's all,' Devon smiled excusingly. 'He does only have an office job, remember.'

'Hmm ... I suppose there is that to consider,' Violet allowed. Then, with her lips pursing speculatively, 'Although I suspect that wouldn't apply to that fit-looking young man out there with your father if the positions were reversed.'

Devon's aquamarine eyes rounded incredulously. It was such an uncustomary kind of comment for her aunt to make. 'Do you mean Hunt—Hunter ... or whatever his name is?'

'That's right,' was the decisively nodded confirmation. 'That's the one I was referring to—Hunter Kincaid. And if you were talking to them, how is it that you don't know his name?' She fixed her niece with an enquiring gaze. 'Didn't Matt,' the nickname for Devon's father used by just about all his close acquaintances, 'introduce you?'

'Well, no, not exactly,' Devon shrugged evasively. 'You see, I—er—met him during his explorations but we sort of didn't get around to introductions.' As she recollected, at the time she couldn't have cared less about his name! 'Then when we arrived back together Dad just assumed it was only necessary for him to introduce me to Royce Attwood. I merely picked up the Hunt and Hunter from their conversation afterwards.' She began meditatively drying the tomatoes she'd washed. 'In any event, I think you're being a little unfair comparing Garth with someone like that who obviously leads a much more physical, outdoor kind of life as a yacht crewman.' Not only that, but she really would have preferred to try and forget the man entirely!

'Oh, well, if you say so, dear,' her aunt smiled vaguely, her concentration obviously centred on the food again. 'I expect you know your fiancé best.'

As well as Hunter Kincaid by the sound of it! added Devon tartly to herself. He really must have put on a good act in her aunt's presence for that usually so perceptive woman to have been taken in by him to the stage where she was now comparing him favourably against Garth. Previously she had never had anything but praise for Garth's rather studious demeanour, his fastidiousness—and his lack of preoccupation with more athletic pursuits, she recalled a little piquedly.

Whereas, on the other hand, *she* was only too aware just how contemptible Hunter Kincaid could be!

For a while silence reigned in the kitchen as both Devon and her aunt went about their tasks with a minimum of fuss. After so many years of practice they had it down to a fine art now and by the time Garth put in his regular appearance everything was well in hand and they were able to relax a little.

'Oh, hi!' Devon greeted him warmly. With his mid-brown hair slicked back tidily and clad in dark green pants and an oyster-coloured shirt he looked extremely well-groomed, she thought. 'What have you been doing this afternoon?'

'Beginning a new book mainly,' he answered offhandedly as he took a seat by a large antique dresser. 'There didn't appear much choice with you gone and then being informed, civilly but succinctly, that *my* presence wasn't required for the discussion taking place on the verandah.' In a somewhat huffy tone.

It didn't require much for Devon to guess just which discussion he was alluding to, but. . . 'You mean, Dad actually asked you to leave?' she gasped, finding it almost impossible to believe.

'Perhaps not in so many words, but the inference was plain enough!' His rather narrow lips pressed together in patent disapproval. 'And that when I would have thought my presence, more than any other, as the partner in my father's firm who deals with all Cowrie Island's business affairs, would have been imperative if business was to be discussed.'

'Business?' she echoed, even more surprised now than after his last revelation. 'What sort of business?'

'How should I know?' he countered on a now

markedly peeved note. 'I wasn't allowed to hear what was being said!'

Stranger and stranger, pondered Devon confusedly, and half beginning to wish now that she had stayed around a while longer herself in order to have discovered just what was going on. However, to try and mollify her fiancé's obviously injured pride, she tried to dismiss the matter lightly.

'Oh, well, maybe Dad was simply attempting to save you from having to listen to a dreary discourse concerning something he knew would be of no interest to you,' she suggested, albeit rather lamely.

Garth merely gave her another aggrieved look. 'What happens on this island is of interest to me. Not only as your father's accountant, but also as your fiancé.'

From across the room, Violet now glanced at him swiftly. 'But I understood your father was Matt's accountant.'

'Since they've been friends for such a long time, and because he was originally, technically I suppose he still is, Miss Matthews,' he conceded formally, if a little on the fractious side. 'Nevertheless, I'm the one who actually audits the island's books and handles all the paperwork now.'

'I see,' Violet nodded stiffly, taking his touchiness amiss, and it was left to her niece to return the conversation to their original topic.

'So you know no more about the whole matter than we do,' she sighed disappointedly.

'If you also know absolutely nothing, it would appear not,' Garth acceded in clipped accents, clearly still put out by the whole episode.

Devon sighed again. It seemed she was just going

to have to wait for her father to divulge the reasons for his unexpected and uncustomary behaviour after all.

# CHAPTER TWO

THROUGHOUT the meal that evening it was extremely difficult for Devon to stop her increasing curiosity from getting the better of her and begin questioning her father at the table, but as she knew he would never discuss business of any kind in front of their guests she had no choice but to contain herself as best she could.

By the time the guests had been served coffee in the sitting room, however, and her father stated his intention of taking a walk down to the yachties' camp—as he often did in the evenings for a drink and a chat around the camp fire—she could stand it no longer and promptly followed him as he headed for the doorway.

'I'll go with you,' she declared, even though on this occasion she would really have preferred to give it a miss. The less she saw of Hunter Kincaid the better she would like it!

'So will I,' said Garth firmly and earned himself a rather exasperated glance from his fiancée as a result.

If, as he had implied, her father hadn't wanted to discuss the matter in his presence before, it was possible he wouldn't want to now either. Besides, since he had previously always considered a visit to the bottom camp somewhat below his dignity, he was making it too obvious as to why he was willing to make an exception tonight.

'You don't have to if you'd rather not,' she therefore proposed as they reached the steps, hoping he would take the hint. 'I know all that nautical talk doesn't greatly interest you, and I don't expect we'll be away all that long.'

Ignoring the hint—purposely, Devon suspected—Garth kept pace with them doggedly. 'No, that's all right. Perhaps I should take more interest ... in preparation for the time when we're married and I take over the running of the island.'

Devon squirmed inwardly at his choice of words. The idea had been mentioned for them to have a larger say in Cowrie's management but it definitely wasn't a foregone conclusion as yet. 'Yes, well, nothing's actually been formally decided along those lines yet, Garth,' she felt obliged to remind him. 'In any event, the proposal suggested was for *both* of us to take charge,' she emphasised indignantly, 'and then only if Dad decides to relinquish control.'

'But I thought it was all settled that he would be off on this trip he's been planning once his boat is ready,' Garth put forward, his own voice sounding rather resentful now. 'Has that idea been scrapped, then, Mr Matthews?' He looked across to the older man intently.

'There's some who would like to see that happen,' Granville disclosed eloquently, his eyes straying towards Devon.

'And you know very well why!' she retorted. 'You're seventy-one years old, and at your last check-up even your doctor advised you to start taking it easier. Nor do I consider your sailing off on your own on that little boat of yours particularly well-advised!'

'But if that's what he wants to do ...' interposed Garth with a shrug and received a positive glare for his efforts this time.

'That doesn't necessarily make it right!' she snapped. 'I mean, anything could happen, and at sea is quite likely to. It wouldn't be so bad if there was someone with him, but to even contemplate going off completely on one's own on that old boat. . .' She shook her head disbelievingly.

'And if it was in a new one?' Her father crooked a quizzical white brow.

She hunched one shoulder deprecatingly. 'Well, naturally I suppose that would put it in a slightly better light, although I still wouldn't be in favour of it . . . and nor would Aunt Violet,' she added in order to lend more weight to her argument. 'Besides, we all know the island's finances aren't in a position to cover such a purchase so there's not much point in discussing it.'

He exhaled slowly. 'You're probably right,' he allowed, and they continued along the smooth, downward path leading to the island's mooring area in silence, each of them occupied with their own thoughts.

Devon still felt somewhat annoyed regarding both her fiancé's assumption of his role once they were married and his virtually endorsing remarks concerning her father's proposed lone sailing trip around the continent. He knew as well as she did that the doctor had recommended her father not to undertake anything too strenuous from now on, she fumed. Moreover, he was also making it extremely difficult for her to question her father about the events of the afternoon. If he hadn't stubbornly insisted on accompanying them she would have been able to have sought some answers by now instead of having to keep them bottled inside her until an appropriate time presented itself when she could manage to get her father alone!

There were five yachts apart from the Kanandah anchored in the lee of the low promontory that curved westwards, their crews talking desultorily as they sat around a blazing fire—used to provide light rather than heat—in an open area between the trees just a short distance from the beach and the old wooden jetty where the trading launch off-loaded the island's house guests and supplies.

The majority of those present Devon and her father already knew from other visits and were accepted into their midst readily, but Garth was a stranger to all of them and it took a while for the necessary introductions to be completed. When they were finally over and the three of them had been companionably provided with drinks, Devon heaved a sigh of gratitude for having been spared another meeting with one person in particular. In fact, neither of the men she had met that afternoon were present, she noted, and presumed they had chosen to remain aboard for the evening.

No sooner had the general conversation resumed, however, than Devon felt a hand drop lightly on her shoulder and she looked up to find Hunt, his other hand resting similarly on her father's shoulder, bending towards them.

'Mind if I join you?' he enquired smilingly of Granville.

'Please do,' replied the older man genially, already moving in order to make more room for the muscular figure to fit between his daughter and himself—to Devon's irritation. Did he have to be quite so accommodating where this man was concerned? 'Is Royce planning on coming across too?'

'Uh-uh.' Hunt shook his head. 'He retired to his cabin immediately after dinner to do some work. He's got a few notes he wants to make.'

'But you haven't?' hazarded Granville. Disappointedly? wondered Devon in bafflement.

'No, I prefer to keep all my information up here,' laughed Hunt, tapping a finger against his temple. 'Notes can have a habit of getting lost.'

'Isn't that the truth,' Granville averred in a seemingly almost relieved voice that had his daughter's forehead creasing anew as she tried to fathom the reason why her father should be evincing such an emotion—if indeed her suspicion had been correct.

Not that she was allowed much time for her speculations because she now found herself the object of Hunt's somewhat disconcerting attention as his vivid blue eyes took in her puzzled features lazily.

'And how are you tonight, beautiful?' he drawled with just enough taunting humour in his tone to have her pressing her lips together vexedly.

'Do you mean now ... or before you arrived?' she gibed bittersweetly, softly, under cover of the voices surrounding them, and finally managing to dislodge the hand that had still been touching her shoulder.

He merely grinned, his head tilting closer to hers. 'Your animosity is still showing, sweetheart,' he admonished drily in an equally quiet tone. 'And all because I happen to know what you look like unclothed.'

'Which, to my mind, is quite reason enough ... even without your certainly less than gentlemanly behaviour in refusing to leave when it was pointed out—sufficiently succinctly even for you, I would have thought—that your presence was neither wanted nor appreciated!' she muttered vehemently.

'So can I help it if you made such an enchanting picture I was unable to tear my eyes away?' he countered in assumed innocence.

'Yes!' she ground out unequivocally. 'And you can stop referring to the matter all the time as well! Or is that also too much to expect of someone as insensitive as you?' Her arching brows reached an expressive peak.

In return, one of Hunt's own brows lifted sardonically. 'As to that, I guess it would all depend on just how I was *asked*,' he stressed significantly.

His inference was obvious enough and, consequently, did nothing to improve Devon's feelings of resentment. 'And you'll be dead and buried before I ever *ask* anything of you, Hunter Kincaid!' she seethed.

'Even though you've already done so once?'

'When?'

'This afternoon—on the verandah—when I was explaining to your father the reason for your being so—umm—displeased at my intrusion on your privacy. Your eyes, at least, were more than willing to seek my silence then, as I recall,' he reminded on a wry note.

Devon shifted restively. She'd forgotten that! 'A—a favour I more than repaid by keeping quiet myself,' she claimed defensively. 'Because if I had told Dad all that did occur on the beach, I very much doubt he would now be treating you as hospitably as he is doing.'

'Mmm, you could have a point there,' he surprised her by allowing with a slow, rueful smile that had her catching her breath involuntarily. 'Shall we agree to call it quits, then?'

'I fail to see why I should,' she refused his offer of

peace uncharacteristically. Normally she didn't like to prolong disputes of any kind, but for some unaccountable reason she suddenly felt a need, quite distinct from his initial unfavourable impression, to keep this man at a distance. 'You're the one at fault! Besides, since I have no intention of making the mistake of ever being in your vicinity again while you remain on this island, I. . .'

'An intention that could be a little difficult to achieve,' Hunt interposed in a somewhat mocking tone.

Her head lifted challengingly. 'I don't see why.'

'Probably not . . . at the moment.'

'Meaning?' A flicker of apprehension had her staring at him warily. She hadn't liked that significant pause before his last words.

'Cowrie's a relatively small island,' he shrugged. Evasively, she suspected.

'So . . .?'

'It's more than conceivable we could run into each other again.'

'Because of the business you were discussing with Dad?' she chanced a stab in the dark.

'You could say that, I suppose,' he owned, although certainly not as informatively as she could have hoped.

As a result she was forced into debating whether to continue questioning him—which, under the circumstances, went very much against the grain—or to pretend to an indifference she was far from experiencing. Eventually, her desire to know just exactly what was going on overcame her reluctance.

'And just what business would that be?' she queried as nonchalantly as possible.

Before he could reply, however, a voice sounded on her other side. 'If it's not too much to ask, Devon, do you think you could possibly spare me some of your attention also?' Garth put in a little irritably.

Devon could have hit him in her frustration at his inappropriate timing, and something of her annoyance must have shown on her face because Hunt promptly grinned. An action that had her swiftly turning her back to him—just in case he mistakenly believed her aggravation had come about because she preferred talking to him—and forcing an apologetic smile on to her lips for her fiancé's benefit.

'I'm sorry, Garth. I didn't realise we'd been talking so long,' she said contritely.

'Obviously!' he sniffed. 'So just what were the two of you whispering about?'

'Oh, we weren't whispering,' she denied with a light, and hopefully convincing, half laugh. 'We just weren't talking loudly, that's all.'

He grimaced, but didn't press the point. 'Well, what were you discussing so quietly, then?'

'As it so happens, I was attempting to discover what he and Mr Attwood were talking to Dad about this afternoon——' she said, carefully omitting to mention the earlier part of their conversation.

'And?'

'You interrupted me at the most relevant moment,' she relayed with a meaningful grimace.

'How could I have done?' His expression registered his disbelief. 'You'd been talking to him for God knows how long before then!'

'Yes, well, I was attempting to worm my way around to it,' she parried.

Garth uttered a disparaging snort. 'What on earth for? You're entitled to know, aren't you? So why waste time beating about the bush?'

'Because I considered that was the best approach to take, and as it worked out, I'm sure I was right.' Pausing, she chewed at her lip thoughtfully. 'Even then I wasn't exactly given any direct answers. In fact, he was quite uncommunicative.'

'Oh?' His brown eyes narrowed suspiciously. 'So there is something going on that we should know about.'

Devon gazed at him askance. 'I'm not sure how you came to that conclusion. After all, I'm certain Dad's not being deliberately secretive. He just hasn't had an opportunity to mention anything about it yet.'

'Hasn't he?' Garth clearly thought otherwise. 'Then why was I summarily dismissed from the verandah this afternoon, eh?'

Mmm, there was that to consider. 'Oh, I don't know!' She shook her head defeatedly. 'Maybe because. . .' She came to an abrupt halt as a sudden recollection came to mind. 'I wonder if Royce Attwood has any connection with the boat-building industry,' she mused. 'I mean, I thought it was a strange remark for Dad to have made when he mentioned something about a new boat on the way down here, and that would definitely explain why he didn't want you present at their discussion. He knew you'd tell Aunt Violet and myself about it and that we'd both try and talk him out of it. Yes, that's got to be it!' Her voice strengthened with conviction. 'He's considering buying a new boat for that damned trip of his!'

'Oh, well, in that case there's nothing to worry about,' Garth shrugged, noticeably relaxing. 'Although I don't know where the money's supposed to be coming from. The island's barely in credit as it is.'

Devon's mouth levelled exasperatedly. 'Of course there's something to worry about!' she contradicted, concentrating on his first indifferent statement. It wasn't the island's finances that concerned her, it was her parent's health. 'If he did somehow manage to get himself a new boat there'd be no stopping him from going off on his own.'

'A decision for him to make, surely,' proposed Garth negligently. 'Besides, he's always seemed to me to be very capable with boats.'

'Oh, naturally he is!' she retorted in impatient tones. 'Good lord, why wouldn't he be? He's been sailing in them ever since he was old enough to walk! But in case it's escaped your notice, it's rather difficult to be capable if you have a heart seizure or something similar!'

'That's still no reason for you to be sarcastic,' he complained on a rather querulous note. 'That achieves absolutely nothing, and particularly when there's no guarantee he'll suffer anything of the kind anyway.'

Devon made a determined effort to moderate her tone somewhat. 'All right, I'm sorry, but I happen to be very concerned about him, while you don't even appear to care.'

'Only because I think you're making mountains out of molehills,' he offered appeasingly.

Was she? Devon wasn't so certain. After all, she spent more time with her father than anyone else did, and during the last couple of years especially she'd noticed a sad but inescapable deterioration in his physical ability. Not that it was entirely unexpected at his age, and if he hadn't wanted to go off on his sailing trip she doubtlessly would just have accepted it, but as it was she felt *someone* needed to sound a warning regarding the inherent dangers in such a proposal in the hope of dissuading him.

Presently, a few of those around the camp fire began drifting back to their boats; a couple because they planned to leave on the early morning tide—at low water the passage through the reef was still navigable, but not quite so comfortable; others because they wanted to be up early in order to effect repairs or just generally check over their equipment before heading off for a day's fishing on the outer reef.

Of course, immediately the exodus began, Garth was anxious to do likewise, this evening's venture down to the camp obviously not having interested him any more than his previous few had done, and nor had he made any effort to lower his dignity sufficiently to the stage where he would voluntarily participate in any of the discussions. Devon also rose to her feet automatically, preparing to accompany him, despite the fact that she would rather have stayed in the hope of hearing just what Hunt and her father had been deliberating upon for the latter part of the evening.

'We're off now, Dad,' she cut in on their discourse. And in an endeavour to separate him from his companion, 'Are you coming too?'

'No, love, not just yet. I'll be along shortly,' he replied. 'You go with Garth and I'll see you in the morning, okay?'

She sighed and nodded, not really having any option but to agree, and with Garth at her side, turned to leave. As she did so a tall, dark-haired girl emerged from the group on the other side of the fire, her voluptuous figure accentuated by the bikini top and brief shorts she was wearing. Pauline Telfer! Devon grimaced, and it wasn't hard to guess in whose direction she was headed. Along with her brother, the other girl had been a regular visitor to the island for quite some years and one whom Devon knew well. She also blatantly sought, and more often than not received, the attention of all the yachtsmen camped there, and right at present Devon didn't doubt that Hunter Kincaid was the magnet drawing the older girl towards the opposite side of the fire.

A last glimpse over her shoulder as she and Garth began making their way up the track proved her assumption correct as she saw the green-eyed beauty sink down with a feline grace beside Hunt—or should that have been, on top of him? she amended, for Pauline couldn't possibly have moved any closer if she'd tried. Unknowingly angling her head higher, Devon returned her attention to the path leading up to the house. They were probably perfectly matched, she decided sourly, since they both possessed identical characteristics in that they were so self-assured as to be insufferable, and patently never gave a thought to anyone but themselves and their own wishes!

On reaching the house they found it in darkness except for the dim hall and verandah lights that were kept on throughout the night for the benefit of the guests, most of whom always retired early, and entering quietly they proceeded to the door of Devon's room.

'You know, I can't take to that Hunter chap,' Garth caught her unawares by abruptly declaring. 'There's something about him—perhaps it's the way he has of looking at you, mockingly arrogant it seems—but whatever it is, he just rubs me the wrong way.'

'Mmm, I know the feeling.' Devon's lips twisted wryly.

'You don't like him either?'

'Now that you mention it, no, not particularly.'

'I'm glad,' he smiled thankfully. 'For a while there tonight I thought you may have been interested in him.'

'Oh, don't be an idiot,' she reproved with a soft laugh. 'How could I possibly become engaged to someone like you and then be interested in someone like him? You're completely opposite types, and his I would need to be mad to want to have anything to do with. He's vexing, goading, and just plain detestable on occasion as well!'

'Is that so? Well, if you find him being the same again, you just let me know. I'll soon put a stop to that,' he vowed. 'Not that I expect he'll ever get up to the house again. Your father can't possibly have become that friendly with him that he would issue another invite.'

'I certainly hope not,' she seconded on a fervent note. Although if he did, she wasn't sure just how her fiancé would be able to keep his promise should it become necessary. She suspected that there would be nothing at all Garth could do to alter any chosen course of action of Hunter Kincaid's.

'And having got that settled, I guess I'd better say good night,' he murmured, and bending his head, touched his mouth gently to hers.

Devon responded to the slight pressure mechanically rather than spontaneously as her thoughts wandered. Whenever he kissed her Garth was always very proper and controlled, she reflected—somewhat like her Aunt Violet—but at least it meant she was never subjected to any unbidden roaming hands, whereas in the same situation she could well imagine Hunt's hands being extremely exploratory, and no doubt proficiently so too. Abruptly she gulped at the disconcerting turn her thoughts had taken, but fortunately Garth didn't appear to notice anything amiss as he raised his head and smiled.

'So what shall we do tomorrow? Have you anything planned?' he asked.

Recovered now, Devon hunched a slender shoulder offhandedly. 'Well, I've got some designs and so forth for the craft shop in Northport that I have to pack ready for the launch when it arrives in the afternoon, and of course I'll have to be present when it comes in so I can help Dad bring the stores up, as well as make certain the guests who are departing haven't left anything behind. There's four of them going back tomorrow, actually. The rest of my time should be free though. So what do you say to a visit to the waterfall slide? It's a while since you've been there and it's usually fun.'

'Oh, all right,' he acceded, albeit not very enthusiastically. 'I suppose I can always take a book along to read if it becomes too tiring.'

Devon's lips twitched irrepressibly. Him and his books! She enjoyed reading herself, particularly in the evenings, but Garth never went anywhere without arming himself with a variety of reading material beforehand. 'Okay, I'll see you at breakfast, then.'

He nodded, and dropping a last chaste kiss to her brow began making his way towards his own room.

Close to an hour later Devon was still wide awake, her mind so active as to make sleep impossible as she subconsciously awaited her father's return. She just *had* to know for certain what his discussion with Royce Attwood had entailed—if only to hopefully

prove her own worrying assumption wrong!
Consequently, the moment she heard him mounting
the steps she hastily covered her short nightdress with
a cotton wrapper and opened one of the french doors
leading from her room to the verandah.

'Dad, can we have a talk, please?' she enquired
anxiously.

Turning in her direction, Granville nodded slightly,
a wry half smile catching at his lips. 'Mmm, I rather
thought you might be wanting to,' he conceded.

His words had Devon's throat constricting. So there
was something going on! With barely suppressed
apprehension she waited for him to be seated on the
upright chair at her work desk while she perched
herself on the end of the bed.

'You're curious as to my discussions with Royce and
Hunt,' he stated rather than asked.

'Just a little,' she smiled faintly. Not so much
Hunt, of course, since he only appeared to be one of
the crew, but Royce definitely!

He rubbed the tips of his fingers across his forehead
a couple of times, then expelled a long, slow breath.
'They're interested in buying the island,' he disclosed
bluntly.

Devon's eyes flew wide open in shock. That was
something she hadn't even remotely considered! His
'they're interested' only registering briefly. 'But—
you've no intention of selling, though, have you?' she
queried nervously, even as she tried to persuade
herself such an eventuality was totally unthinkable.
When all was said and done, there had been similar
offers in the past that had been refused.

He moved one shoulder in a non-committal gesture.
'They're talking of a seven figure sum, and it would

certainly mean all of us, including you and Garth, would never have any financial worries again.'

The monetary aspect of it Devon discounted immediately. There were other things more important than that. 'But this is our home! It always has been!' she protested. 'And as for Garth and myself, when the time comes what's wrong with us just continuing to run the guesthouse as our family's always done?'

'For you, maybe nothing, you're used to living out here, but Garth isn't, and of late I'm afraid I've begun to have my doubts as to whether he's capable of keeping the place going,' he sighed.

'Oh, of course he is!' she claimed defensively. 'In fact, with his qualifications as an accountant, I'd have thought he was perfect for the position of manager.'

'For balancing the books, he no doubt is,' Granville agreed. 'However, as you know full well, that isn't all he would be required to do, and that's what has me worried.'

'Such as?'

'Firstly, since it hardly makes for a cordial atmosphere, he would need to modify that somewhat distant attitude he shows towards the guests at times. . .'

'Well, naturally he would once they were his responsibility,' she inserted persuasively.

'And secondly,' he continued, 'his apparent aversion to physical activity of just about any kind doesn't particularly augur well for his keeping the place in running order when there's the jetty constantly needing repairs to retain it in even moderately serviceable order; the gardens to be attended to; the generators maintained; the house repainted regularly; the motorboat kept in good order since that's our only private means of reaching the mainland; general household repairs to be effected; plus a hundred and one other things that crop up from time to time, all of which involve physical exertion.' He held up a hand when she would have spoken. 'Oh, I know what you're going to say—that he'll change when he realises it's up to him to attend to all these matters—but unfortunately I'm beginning to wonder if he will. I find it more likely that after a few months or so he'll either be leaving most of the work to *you*, or else he'll be wanting to hire someone to do it for him. The first prospect is one I intend to do my utmost to see never occurs, and the second is one which could possibly mean the difference between the island making a profit, even though small, and a loss.'

'That's still no reason for considering selling the place!' Devon burst out anguishedly. 'And if I'm prepared to take a chance with Garth I don't see why you shouldn't be too! You can't be certain that's what's going to happen.'

Granville sighed, his expression sympathetically understanding. 'No, that's true enough, but at my age I think I do have a little more experience with regard to human nature than you do, love, and in this case can perhaps see matters with slightly more objectivity.'

Devon bit at her lip disconsolately, her breathing deep and disturbed. 'But I don't want to see the island sold—to have to leave here—and nor will Aunt Violet,' she all but choked. It was just too dispiriting to contemplate!

'Yes—well—nothing's been finalised as yet, of course. They're also only considering it at the moment. It could take weeks before a decision is actually made, and then only if it's acceptable to all concerned.'

He was attempting to make it sound less of a foregone conclusion, she knew, but the fact that he was really considering it did little to offer encouragement and her expression remained despondent.

'Anyway, just who did you mean when you said *they're* interested in buying the island?' she questioned moodily. 'I thought Hunt was one of the *Kanandah*'s crew.'

To her surprise, and resentment that he could find something humorous at such a stage, her father chuckled. 'Whatever gave you that idea?'

Did that mean he wasn't? 'Well, he dresses like he is, and he sure doesn't behave any better than some of the rougher ones we've had call in here,' she grimaced.

'Oh? What makes you say that?'

Her turquoise eyes flashed stormily. If she could only tell him precisely! 'Because he couldn't—or most probably, wouldn't!—even apologise for disturbing me this afternoon, and—and he's done nothing but goad me about the incident ever since . . . as if I was the one in the wrong!' she had to be satisfied with complaining indignantly instead.

To her added annoyance he appeared to take no exception to hearing that. 'Your reception of him having been impeccable, of course,' he merely put forward drily.

Her chin lifted defiantly. 'I don't know what you mean.'

'Maybe not, but I certainly know *you*, love, and what your reaction usually is when someone chances exploring this side of the island.'

The same as his had been until today! 'Then

perhaps you should have remembered that before giving him permission to look over the beach,' she returned huffily.

'I did,' he laughed. 'But Hunt assured me he'd be able to handle the situation, and . . .' he sent her a teasing glance, 'it would appear he succeeded.'

All too well! recalled Devon, her cheeks warming involuntarily at the memory. 'Yes—well—in any event, that's neither here nor there,' she shrugged dismissively. Not surprisingly, the main origin of her resentment wasn't something she wanted to dwell on. 'Then if he isn't one of the crew, just who is he?'

Her father's mouth tilted wryly. 'He's Chairman of the Board of the Eastern Development Corporation.'

Momentarily, Devon stared at him in stunned silence, and then she was shaking her head in disbelief. 'According to whom? Him?' She gave a lightly sardonic laugh. 'I think you're being taken for a ride, Dad. He couldn't possibly be Chairman of a Board. He's not old enough for a start.'

'He has all the evidence necessary to prove it, as does Royce,' her father shrugged. 'And I put a call through to Brisbane this afternoon in order to check the ownership of the *Kanandah*. It's registered to Eastern Developments, all right.'

On the surface it appeared convincing, and yet. . . 'And they just happened to be cruising around here when they decided they wanted to buy an island, did they?' she scoffed.

He half smiled at her vehemence and shook his head. 'No, as a matter of fact they have a report with them—which I found perhaps most conclusive of all—that had been submitted by one of their own project engineers some three or four months ago, in which it was recommended that the island be studied in depth with a view to purchase and development,' he relayed. Then, with his brows raised enquiringly, 'Do you remember that nice young feller who was crewing on that big ocean-racing yacht that called in here. The— the. . .' He snapped his fingers impatiently as he tried to remember the name.

'The *Drifter*, you mean?' she supplied swiftly.

'Mmm, that was the name of it,' he nodded. 'And you remember the feller I'm talking about too, don't you?'

'Oh, yes, I remember Dean Henderson,' she confirmed with some asperity. Up until then she'd thought of him as being rather pleasant, but now she positively loathed him! 'So that was why he was up here asking all those questions, was it?'

'Apparently—and the reason for the *Kānandah* being in these waters now.'

'I see.' She pulled a disgruntled face. 'And Royce Attwood? Who's he, then? And how come you were doing most of your talking with him?'

'I understand he's Hunt's executive director, and the reason I was discussing the matter with him mostly was because, at this stage at least, Hunt was more interested in actually seeing something of the island for himself.' He paused, eyeing her watchfully. 'He also wants to undertake a thorough exploration of the whole island, as well as its special features, starting tomorrow morning, and I said I thought you'd be the best person to show it to him,' he concluded in something of a rush.

'No way!' Devon ejaculated in horrified accents. 'I can't—I won't do it, Dad! That's as good as asking me to help sell it!' She gazed at him with a hurt expression. 'Besides, I don't even like the man. Why can't he simply go looking on his own if he's so keen to see it? He didn't seem to have any objections to doing that this afternoon! Or why can't you show him? You certainly appear to get on well enough with him.' A hint of bitterness edged its way into her voice.

'I do,' he averred quietly. 'In fact, I happen to like him very much. He's down to earth, he lays it straight on the line without giving you any bull, he's done his homework on the subject, and he's got a great sense of humour.'

'A veritable prince among men, in fact,' she gibed acidly.

A remark that was studiously ignored. 'Nevertheless, as much as I'm sure I would enjoy his company while showing him what we have here, I suspect that these days you're more knowledgeable and definitely more capable—no doubt he'd like to go snorkelling over the reef, and you know I haven't done any of that for years—in that regard than I am, hence my suggestion that you accompany him.'

She sucked in a deep breath. 'And if—if I refuse?' she hazarded shakily, unable to recall the last time she had even contemplated . not fulfilling one of her father's requests.

'He'll doubtless manage to see it all, anyhow.' Halting, he glanced down at the floor for a moment, then brought his gaze deliberately back to hers. 'While we both know who'll be the losers, don't we?'

Devon half turned away, pressing her lips together dejectedly. She didn't want him to be disappointed in her, or in herself either for that matter, as she knew she unquestionably would be in the months to come if she didn't accede to his request, but at the same time she felt she had to at least attempt to forestall the inevitable somehow.

'I—I've made arrangements to go to the waterfall with Garth in the morning,' she hedged throatily without looking at him.

The wooden chair creaked as her father left it and walked across to the bed, a work-roughened hand tipping her pensive and misty-eyed face up to his. 'Would it be too much to ask for you to postpone that until the afternoon?' Granville quizzed gently.

She partly spread her hands and then clenched them again in her lap. 'I don't expect there'll be time with the launch arriving.'

'You don't think he would be willing to exchange the waterfall for a few hours' reading?' whimsically.

Despite herself, a rueful smile caught at Devon's wide mouth. 'Probably,' she conceded. As Garth had said, he was planning to take a book along anyway.

'Then you will act as Hunt's guide?'

'Oh, I suppose so,' she sighed resignedly. The look in her eyes suddenly turned urgent. 'If you're sure this is what you really want?'

His fingers lingered softly against her chin for a second before he dropped his hand to his side. 'The only thing I'm sure of at the moment is that I'd like to know all the pros and cons before I make *any* decision,' he assured her. 'That is, of course, apart from being very certain I couldn't possibly love my daughter any more than I do right now, and all I care about is seeing her well provided for, both now and in the future.'

'Oh, Dad!' she cried helplessly. 'You make me feel so ungrateful, and yet all I want is for things to remain the same as they've always been.'

'I know, love, I know,' he smiled fondly. 'But I'm not getting any younger, and sometimes we just have to make the best of things and that includes changes when they come.'

They were words Devon was still turning over in her mind when she returned to her bed after her father had gone, and although she vowed to at least try not to make her father's decision any more difficult than it already obviously would be, where someone else was concerned she felt quite entitled to attempt to influence the outcome—by whatever means she could!

# CHAPTER THREE

THE minute Devon walked into the kitchen the following morning and saw her aunt's thoughtful expression she knew someone else had been there before her.

'Dad's already told you, I gather,' she deduced with a faint half smile.

'He has,' Violet nodded as she continued turning the bacon in the pan on top of the range.

When nothing else appeared to be forthcoming, Devon peered at her more closely. 'And?'

Her aunt shrugged indeterminately. 'Well, I'm not in favour of it, naturally, but it's his right to sell if he so wishes, and ...' she sighed, her lips pursing, 'I must admit I can understand his reasons for considering it—especially since the initial offer is so tempting.'

'Initial offer?' probed Devon curiously.

'Oh, you know how it is, these things are always negotiable. It all depends on the final conditions—ours and theirs,' Violet declared with the knowledge born of other such approaches. 'At this stage you can't even be certain it will come to anything. No doubt they'll want to cost the whole project first—construction of new buildings, improved facilities, faster and more frequent methods of access to and from the mainland, the anticipated number of likely guests and so forth—and only then will it be decided if the deal actually goes through or not.'

Devon touched her teeth to her lower lip in silent contemplation as she began breaking eggs into another pan, her aunt's information surprising her a little. 'Have any previous offers Dad's received reached the costing stage, then?' she questioned. She couldn't remember any herself that had done so.

Violet attended to the steaks already sizzling under the grill before speaking. 'A couple. The most recent while you were away at boarding school, but none of them proceeded any further. When they discovered they couldn't use their costs as a lever for persuading your father into letting the place go for a song they soon disappeared back to where they'd come from.' Pausing, her demeanour turned meditative again. 'As a matter of fact, I rather think that's why he's prepared to be more than usually helpful now to Messrs Attwood and Kincaid. At least it seems they're willing to be fair, and didn't just breeze on to the island as a few others have done and insult his intelligence by treating him like some rustic simpleton who had no idea what the place was worth.'

More or less as her father had intimated the night before, Devon brooded, and on hearing footsteps behind her, turned to find Garth entering the room.

'Morning!' He included them both in his greeting. 'Although I must say you two are looking somewhat pensive today. Anything wrong?'

Since there didn't appear to be any soft way of breaking the news, Devon came out with it flatly. 'Dad's considering selling the island.'

For a second Garth's jaw dropped, so great was his obvious surprise, and then it closed again with a snap. 'But he can't!' he expostulated indignantly. 'What about the plans for us to take over here? Or isn't our future of any importance now? I suppose this is a perfect way for him to get that new boat he's doubtlessly after, is that it?'

Although she didn't doubt such a purchase could be high on her father's list of priorities—if the sale was concluded—Devon was still positive it wouldn't have been a deciding factor in his decision and, as a result, took great exception to her fiancé's unwarranted contention that it had been. Nor did she particularly care for his attitude of apparently only seeing such a sale in the light of how it might affect himself.

'Not as far as I'm aware, no!' she repudiated sharply. 'While as for our future, as it so happens I understand that *was* a major consideration in his decision.'

'Oh!' Some of his indignation began to disappear, but whether because of her last statement, or because of her bristling response, she couldn't be certain. 'You mean, *that's* what he was discussing all yesterday afternoon?' His upper lip curled satirically. 'No wonder he didn't want me around. He knew I would have had something to say about it.'

'In your capacity as the island's accountant?' put in Violet subtly.

A mottled stain coloured his rather pale cheeks. 'Yes—well—in that guise also, I expect,' he blustered. 'After all, it is my place to advise and guide in these matters, and—and I really think my recommendations should have been sought before he consented to discuss whatever proposal has been put to him.' Abruptly, he began to look worried. 'He hasn't signed anything yet, has he? For all we know they could be attempting to rob him blind! Oh, well, even if he has, I'm sure I'll be able to circumvent it somehow.' Sounding considerably more relieved.

'That is, only if Dad wishes you to,' Devon stated succinctly. 'Not that I can imagine him having done anything of the kind so precipitately anyway. He's not exactly senile, you know, Garth.'

'No, no, of course not,' he hastened to placate her. 'I wasn't really intending to imply that he was. It's just that some of these people are very smooth operators, and I don't believe now, with the real estate market as depressed as it is, is the correct time to even be considering selling—as no doubt that Kincaid feller is well aware!' His voice hardened with dislike. 'That's probably what he's banking on. Getting it cheap now and then re-selling it once the market improves, and pocketing the extra profits that should be ours!'

'Well ... Dad's,' she couldn't help amending pointedly. 'In any event, I would hardly call an offer of seven figures attempting to buy it on the cheap.'

'Seven, you said?' Garth queried immediately, his eyes widening. 'And the exact amount?'

'I didn't bother to ask,' she all but flared. She didn't know whether she was being overly sensitive this morning, but to her mind she didn't really think he should have been asking either. 'I wasn't particularly interested. Especially as I hope nothing comes of the whole affair. I'd willingly forgo any financial benefit in order to continue living here. As I'm sure Aunt Violet would too, wouldn't you?' She looked to her relative for corroboration.

'Oh, unquestionably,' that woman promptly concurred with feeling. 'I couldn't imagine living anywhere else now after all these years. It's really become home to me.'

With the last of the hot foods now ladled into covered warming dishes, Devon and her aunt began carrying them through to the dining room where they were placed alongside the fruits and cereals already laid out on a long, polished sideboard. Breakfast and lunch were always casual meals with no stringently set time tables so the guests could arrive as it suited them and help themselves.

Seeing Garth following her, empty-handed, on one such trip, Devon nodded towards the dish filled with triangles of golden toast that was still on the kitchen table.

'Bring that in for me, will you, please, Garth?' she requested. 'It's the only one left.'

'Oh, all right,' he agreed, but to her amazement seeming a trifle aggrieved at having been asked to do something so menial. Then, as he caught up to her again, 'How long do you expect it to take you to pack your designs, etcetera, after breakfast?'

'Not long. Only about fifteen minutes or so,' she replied. The subject suddenly triggered a reminder of her promise to her father—how could she have forgotten!—and she came to a halt just before the dining-room doorway. 'Oh, by the way, I'm very sorry but we can't go to the waterfall, after all. Or at least I can't,' she modified with a grimace. 'Dad's asked me to act as guide for one of our *visitors*,' sardonically, 'on a tour of the island this morning.'

'Which one? Kincaid?' he immediately wanted to know, his tone sour.

She pulled another expressive face. 'Unfortunately!'

'And it has to be this morning? Why not some other time?'

'He apparently wants to see all the island has to offer as soon as possible,' she shrugged.

'In order to provide him with more ideas for making

money out of the place, I suppose!' Garth sneered.
'Well, I think I'll just go along with you. He can't
have any objections to that, can he?'

Considering Hunt's comments regarding her fiancé
the day before, Devon thought it more than likely, and
because of that she found she too was a little reluctant
to have him accompany them. It would be difficult
enough as it was putting up with Hunt on his own,
without having the pair of them needling each other
the whole time as well.

'I wouldn't know, but I'm afraid *I* don't really think
it's such a good idea, Garth,' she owned in as
apologetic a manner as she could. But on seeing him
about to protest, went on hurriedly. 'I mean, it's more
than probable Royce Attwood will be talking to Dad
again today, and surely it's more important for you to
be available to sit in on their discussions.'

'Provided I'm allowed, that is!' pungently.

'Oh, I can't see why you wouldn't be. Not now that
the secret's out, anyway,' she predicted confidently.
'Besides, you know how much you dislike hiking all
over the place, and I intend to set such a pace that he
won't have an opportunity to get more than a passing
glance at anything, and you'd only hate it even more
under those circumstances. Also,' she half smiled
impishly, 'I only mean to show him the worst aspects
of the island in any case. I'm sure not going to make it
easy for him to decide whether Cowrie's suitable for
what he's got in mind.'

'That's the way!' Garth approved with acrid
pleasure. 'If we can't alter your father's attitude,
perhaps we can alter his.'

'Precisely!' Devon nodded in emphasis. 'So while
I'm putting that scheme into action this morning,

you'll stay here and find out what's happening this end with Dad?'

'Mmm, as you say, that's no doubt the best way to play it,' he conceded, and in a mood of complete accord they entered the dining room together.

As soon as the meal was concluded Garth disappeared in search of Granville—who always breakfasted at a much earlier hour in the kitchen—and knowing he would be dogging her father's footsteps for the remainder of the day, Devon couldn't help but smile. Her father's activities had certainly never created such an interest in her fiancé before.

In the meantime she cleaned and tidied the dining room quickly while her aunt attended to the kitchen, and then returned to her bedroom in order to sort and pack her most recent designs in a heavy folder ready for transport to the mainland on the trading launch. She still had a few of them laid out on the bed as she deliberated whether to include them all or not, when there was a knock at the open door that led on to the verandah and on looking round she saw Hunt's tall figure filling the doorway. Dressed similarly to the day before in T-shirt and shorts, he seemed to fill the room with a disturbing aura of unassailable masculinity as he casually ambled inside to take a look at the paintings on the bed.

'Matt said I'd probably find you here,' he said lazily. 'You wouldn't be trying to avoid our little tour of the island, would you?'

Confused slightly, both by his nonchalant entrance and his presence that seemed to totally dominate the femininely decorated room her father had been the only male to enter previously, Devon backed away a few steps in an effort to lessen the feeling of being helplessly overwhelmed.

'N-no, of course not. Why would I do that?' she countered, if a little jerkily. 'I—I was just getting these ready,' she rushed to gather up the colourfully patterned sheets of paper, 'for the boat this afternoon, that's all.'

'I see.' His attractively shaped mouth curved wryly, and before she could stop him he calmly removed the designs from her suddenly lifeless fingers and began spreading them out on her bed once more. 'What are they for?'

'S-souvenir designs,' she stammered—much to her annoyance that she should be permitting him to affect her so. 'I sell them to a shop in Northport.'

'They're very good,' he commended, continuing to peruse them intently. 'I like that one in particular,' Pointing to a palm-silhouetted sunset. And slanting her a quizzical gaze, 'Have you ever done any solely promoting the island?'

She hunched a darkly golden shoulder diffidently. 'I did a couple for some ashtrays and tea towels once, but most of our guests aren't the type to go in for T-shirts, sarongs, beach towels, and that sort of thing.'

'Although you could devise some exclusive designs if there was a market for them?'

'I guess so if . . .' She halted, suddenly realising the direction of his thoughts. '*If* I felt like it,' she stressed meaningfully. She was damned if she'd help promote the island for his benefit when it meant she wouldn't be able to live there any more!

Hunt merely grinned and turned his attention to the wall beside her bed while Devon hastily re-gathered her paintings once again. 'You also do murals, I see,' he mused.

Glancing up involuntarily, she surveyed the brightly coloured scene of various corals and sea life she had painted the year before, and which his eyes were now ranging over measuringly. 'Not really,' she denied. 'That's the only one I've ever done and I've never really been satisfied with it.'

'Why not? It looks extremely life-like to me.'

Deliberately excluding the design Hunt had said he'd liked, although she wasn't at all certain just why she retained it, Devon added the rest to the folder and began tying its securing cords. 'Oh, the giant clam isn't quite in proportion, and there's just something wrong with the Imperial Angel fish,' she relayed absently.

'Which one's that?' he smiled down at her drily.

Discovering her own lips to be waywardly curving in response, she clamped them together determinedly and busied herself with inserting the folder within its special waterproof covering. 'The one with the purple and black markings on its head, and royal blue and yellow striped body,' she advised coolly.

'I can't see anything wrong with it,' he declared after a few moments.

'Mmm, but then you didn't even know which one it was either, did you?' she quipped sardonically.

'Which just goes to show how much there is for you to teach me.'

At that, Devon's head lifted swiftly. 'What do you mean ... teach you?' she demanded, startled. 'Dad only asked me to show you over the island. Nothing else!'

'You could also impart a little information along the

way, though, couldn't you?' His vivid blue eyes met hers mockingly.

In defence, she half turned away on the pretext of sealing the folder's cover. 'What makes you think any such information I might give you would be the truth? I'm not at all interested in seeing the island sold, you know.'

'So Matt said, but I still think I'll back my own judgment as to when you're telling the truth and when you're not.' He paused, a lopsided smile pulling at his lips. 'Matt also warned me you could be tempted to try something of the sort.'

Oh, had he? She was beginning to wonder just whose side her father was on! That was also the second time he had referred to her parent as Matt—something Garth still hadn't been invited to do as yet!—and the fact that her father appeared to have accepted this man—of all people—so willingly, and so readily, infuriated her. But that very same anger did at least enable her to now face him challengingly.

'Then if you would care to put your judgment to the test, Mr Kincaid. . .' Leaving the folder on the bed she indicated the door with an outspread hand.

'Hunt,' he corrected drily without moving.

Since that was how she already thought of him, it seemed rather senseless not to comply, even though she considered there was perhaps more reason for keeping him at a distance now than there had been yesterday. 'Very well, then,' she consented primly. 'So now shall we go?'

'After you, beautiful,' he drawled. 'We've got a lot of ground to cover out there.'

And all of which she would see they did so in as short a time as possible, she vowed as she stepped out on to the verandah and began leading the way around to the steps at the back of the house and then across the lawn to a different track from the one they had used the day before.

'Where are we going first?' Hunt queried indolently as he followed her in among the leafy vegetation.

'I thought we'd take this walking track right through to the seaward side and then make our way back around the perimeter of the island from there,' Devon disclosed without turning to look at him. Mostly in order to hide the pleasurable twinkle evident in her eyes. First impressions always seemed to make the greatest impact, so where better to start than the least imposing areas.

As they passed she reeled off some of the names of the trees, although only the exotic ones he wasn't likely to remember, as well as some of the birds her accustomed eyes picked up among the branches. However, after only travelling a few hundred yards, she disappointingly found her rapid pace beginning to slow as the heat of the day—January was always their hottest month—made it impossible even for her, as used to it as she was, to keep it up for too long, and when they reached the point where another track branched to the left of their own and Hunt determinedly brought her to a halt by catching hold of her arm, she wasn't entirely sorry.

'Hold it, sweetheart!' he ordered wryly. 'Where does that lead to?'

'Only The Pinnacle,' she revealed in as unsinterested a tone as possible.

'Which provides a view of the whole of the island?'

'In a manner of speaking.'

'Meaning?' He eyed her speculatively from beneath narrowed lids.

'Only that it's not really high enough to give a decent view,' she lied. In truth, the view from the top was nothing short of breathtaking—and the very reason she didn't want it to be the first place they visited. The fact that there were two sailors' graves—crew members from the ship that gave Careen Beach its name early in the previous century—to inspect along the route, as well as a cave filled with Aboriginal paintings from an even earlier period, she conveniently forgot to mention at all. She merely shrugged and proposed, 'You could always go up there some other time, if you really wanted to. You don't need me to show it to you.'

For a brief moment she didn't. think he intended taking her word for it as he looked along the branching path interestedly, and her heart raced, but then to her immeasurable relief he gave a faint smile and indicated they should continue along the track she had originally chosen.

After the short, somewhat cooling rest, Devon set off again as fast as she could, but this time Hunt wasn't waiting until something of interest caught his attention before bringing her to a stop, and no sooner had she gone a few yards than a hand gripped the nape of her neck and effectively brought her to a standstill.

'Okay, sweetheart, you've had your fun,' he drawled. 'Now just let's take it a bit slower, shall we? I'd like to at least take note of something while we're on this little jaunt.'

'Oh, I am sorry if I was going too fast for you. I forgot you're probably more used to travelling everywhere by car,' she apologised, provokingly tongue-in-cheek. 'It's just that I have to get back to help Aunt Violet with the lunch, you see.'

'No, you don't. Matt said he'd help out in the kitchen if you weren't back in time,' he both surprised and irritated her by advising. Her father's co-operation was becoming hard to believe—and even harder to take! 'Nor were you going too fast for me. I'd simply appreciate taking in the scenery a little more. If you have no objections, that is?' His dark head tilted enquiringly, tauntingly.

'Not at all,' she pretended, grimacing inwardly at having her plan partially thwarted. 'Does this suit you better?' She set off once more, but at a veritable snail's pace on this occasion.

'All right! If that's the way you want it!'

There was some nuance in Hunt's voice that had her about-facing warily, and just in time to see him bend before she was slung unceremoniously over a broad shoulder, a bronzed and sinewed arm wrapping around her bare legs, ensuring she remained there. With a muffled cry of surprise and outrage, Devon immediately began to pound clenched fists against his muscular back.

'How dare you! Put me down this instant, you damned great ape!' she half demanded, half panted as he resumed walking—at a normal speed. 'Put me down this instant, do you hear?' Her voice rose wrathfully.

'I hear,' he averred drily, the predominantly amused tone only enraging her further.

'Well, then?' she heaved impatiently, her pummelling action growing weaker as her arms started to tire.

'I'll put you down when you promise to behave, and when you *ask* instead of commanding me to do so . . . not before!' came the decisive return.

'*Ask* to be put down!' she flared. 'Why should I? I didn't *ask* to be treated so—so barbarously!'

'Didn't you?' he countered lazily. 'I figured you did.'

'You would! You obviously don't know any better, you—you. . . .' She broke off as the breath was knocked out of her when he effortlessly jumped a shallow gully that crossed the path, but promptly resumed once they were back on to even ground. 'I knew immediately I set eyes on you yesterday that you were nothing but an inconsiderate, insensitive. . . . Ouch!' A none too gentle slap on her behind had her crying out resentfully.

'Then be quiet,' she was directed on a sardonic note. 'It would be an enjoyable walk if it wasn't for your squawking.'

Her *squawking*! About to begin another tirade, Devon suddenly thought better of it. Against someone like him it obviously wouldn't have any effect, and apart from that, since every step he took jolted her stomach unmercifully she was only making it worse for herself by continuing.

'All right! *Please* put me down!' she was finally forced into requesting.

To her relief that at least had him stopping, although he didn't immediately make any move to release her. 'And are you going to behave, instead of acting like a peevish, spoilt brat?'

'Oh, yes, anything, but just put me down,' she pleaded. It would be altogether too much to bear if they happened to come across some of the island's guests while she was in such a mortifying position.

'Anything?' Dark brows rose graphically above taunting blue eyes as he finally consented to do as she wished, but without fully relinquishing his hold on her as his encircling arms held her loosely, but discomposingly, close to his rugged frame.

Flustered, and unable to answer in kind as a result, Devon broke away from him resentfully. 'God, I hate you!' she gritted. 'I wish you'd never come here! You really think you're a law unto yourself, don't you?'

'Because I refused to passively submit to your contrary little antics?' Up went those expressive brows of his again.

'Because although you may have managed to ingratiate yourself with my father, that doesn't give you the right to mistreat and humiliate me as and when you feel like it!'

'Not even when it's deserved?'

She noticed he hadn't denied it! 'According to whom . . . you?' she countered scornfully. 'Considering your behaviour has been nothing short of disgraceful ever since you arrived, I wouldn't have thought you were in a position to criticise anyone else's!'

His firmly moulded mouth slanted mockingly. 'Except for a certain, obviously over-indulged young female who likes to give out with the orders, of course.'

'Where you're concerned, why wouldn't I?' she sniped. 'And as for my being over-indulged—I certainly am not! However, if that's the way you feel, no doubt you'd prefer to continue your explorations without me.' She spun on her heel and started back towards the house.

'Oh, no, you don't sweetheart!' A hand on her arm brought her up short. 'You agreed to be my guide, and my guide you're going to be.' He tapped a finger against her chin aggravatingly. 'Even if I have to resort to carrying you again.'

He would too, the brute! she fumed silently, railing against the knowledge that she really had no option but to continue with him. Dragging free of his grip, she glared at him impotently. 'Well, come on, then!' she heaved in patent dissatisfaction as she began heading along the track once more. 'I haven't got all day!'

'Your fiancé's anxiously awaiting your return, is he?' came the drawling enquiry from behind her.

'Why wouldn't he be?' she half turned to retort with some asperity. 'After all, we did have plans of our own for this morning!'

'For example . . .?'

Her head lifted fractionally higher, but this time she didn't turn. 'That's our business, not yours!'

'You could have brought him along with us . . . or didn't you want to?'

Now Devon did swing round, rapidly. 'I don't know just what you're trying to imply by that, but you can forget it, whatever it is!' He couldn't possibly think she had *wanted* to be alone with him, could he? 'The reason Garth isn't accompanying us is because he has more important things to do.'

'Such as keeping close to Matt in case he has any more discussions with Royce?' surmised Hunt drily on catching up to her.

She dropped her gaze discomfitedly. His deduction had been too shrewd for her liking, and she really wasn't certain she wanted to admit as much. 'What makes you think that?' she parried therefore.

'Probably because he comes across as the type who has his eyes open for the main chance all the time, and right at the moment I don't doubt he's got the wind up at the thought of his inheritance, via you, disappearing,' he contended on a wry note.

Devon's glance flashed back up to his irately. 'That's not true, and how dare you even suggest such a thing! He just doesn't want to see the island sold, that's all. The same as I don't.'

'Well, not at present, and by your father, at any rate. Once the two of you are married, and he has more say, I suspect it would be an entirely different proposition.'

Devon's anger escalated uncontrollably in spite of the sudden remembrance of Garth claiming now wasn't the time to sell. Did that mean, as her companion had just claimed so obnoxiously, that he wouldn't be averse to doing so at some other time? She gave herself a mental shake. No, of course it hadn't meant that. The man beside her was simply attempting to make her believe it was.

'Oh, yes, you'd like me to think that, wouldn't you?' she jeered contemptuously. 'Setting me against my fiancé would unquestionably suit *your* plans admirably. It's called driving a split between the opposition, isn't it?' She halted momentarily, her breasts rising and falling rapidly beneath her thin cotton top. 'How would you know anything about Garth, or his thoughts, anyway? You've only spoken to him once!' Apart from a nodded acknowledgment there definitely hadn't been any communication between the two of them last night at the camp.

Hunt's lips quirked half wryly, half derogatorily. 'And as I said yesterday . . . that was enough.'

Just his expression was sufficient to have her inhaling wrathfully. 'Due to your being such an infallible mind reader, I suppose?' she scoffed in acid tones.

'No, just practised in dealings of this nature, and consequently wise as to just how avaricious some people can be,' he shrugged casually. 'We meet all kinds in our line of work.'

'And so do I here on the island ... witness yourself,' she smiled with sweet sarcasm.

'Mmm, most of whom you pass a few pleasantries with during their week or so's visit and that's the sum total of your knowledge of them. Hardly a sound basis for judging a person's character, would you say?' he goaded. 'In fact, you've lived such a sheltered and secluded life here that I wouldn't mind betting Garth Wilkinson is the only male under the age of fifty you've ever really been associated with, and that merely because his father's firm has been handling the island's affairs for the last thirty years or more.'

'Oh, that's ridiculous!' she rejected his suggestion disdainfully. 'Naturally I've met other young men. The bottom camp is usually full of them.'

'Except I didn't claim you'd never *met* any, just that you'd never associated with another one for any length of time. So tell me ...' he invited, his head tilting quizzically, his thickly lashed eyes alive with a bantering light, 'just how many of these other younger men have you ever become involved with—in a romantic sense, shall we say?'

Unconsciously, Devon's steps faltered a little. 'I— well—none really, I guess,' honesty forced her into conceding, albeit with extreme reluctance. But on catching sight of the satisfied smile beginning to pull at the edges of his shapely mouth, promptly defended, 'Not that that means anything, anyhow, and—and especially where Garth is concerned!'

'It hasn't exactly provided you with the experience

to make a valid comparison either, though, has it?' he asserted drily.

'It's only you who's ever suggested I should do so, and we both know your reasons for wanting me to doubt him now, don't we?' it was her turn to mock. 'It would make matters so much more simple for you with my father, wouldn't it?'

Hunt flexed a wide shoulder dispassionately. 'I wasn't aware Matt either needed your consent, or even a lack of opposition on your part, in order to make his decision.'

Devon abruptly caught at her lower lip with even white teeth to halt its dismayed trembling. Unfortunately, he was all too correct. 'How thoughtful of you to remind me,' she quipped in throaty tones. 'That must really have made your day.'

'No, far from it, as a matter of fact.' He raked a hand through his hair irritably as his gaze rested on her despondent profile. 'And I'm sorry. It was a tactless remark to have made under the circumstances. Believe it or not, I can understand why you're so against a change in the status quo here.'

Although her eyes had flickered briefly in his direction on hearing him apologise—that was definitely something she hadn't anticipated—they were now firmly fixed to the track again. 'Nevertheless, anything so unproductive as personal feelings won't be allowed to stand in your way, of course,' she disparaged.

He gave a rueful half laugh. 'With the potential I believe this place to have, I couldn't afford to.'

'Ah, yes, I was forgetting the quest for the almighty dollar, wasn't I? It means everything to the likes of you, doesn't it?'

'Does it?' For the first time she detected something

of a bite in his voice rather than its customary drawling indolence. 'I see it more as providing a location many can enjoy instead of merely a few ... *if* it's decided to go ahead and purchase it, that is!'

So there was still some hope, noted Devon in relief, her step becoming infinitesimally lighter as they approached the low dunes denoting the end of the path. 'But it's my *home!*' she still lamented. 'And it's not as if there aren't dozens of other islands on the reef people can visit. I would have thought the market was saturated with them already.'

'Sorry, but our surveys indicate otherwise,' he contradicted, but this time without sounding at all apologetic. 'Particularly for the kind of resort we envisage.'

'Huh! One with music blaring continuously, the day organised from beginning to end, and an elaborate swimming pool surrounded by artificial grass no doubt just so guests can lounge around a garish complex without actually having to be—ghastly thought!—contaminated by the salt and the sand, I suppose,' she derided.

'Vixen!' he surprised her by grinning as he gave a lock of her blonde hair a lightly punishing tug. 'Actually, it's just the opposite. My thoughts are to make a true "get away from it all" resort where people can really unwind by leaving it in as natural a state as possible, but with better service and accommodation available, as well as providing the necessary facilities for a greater range of activities for those who do wish to participate in them.'

'Such as?' she probed, curious in spite of trying not to be.

'Oh, scuba diving, sail-boarding, fishing excursions, trips to the outer reef, ski paddling, that kind of thing,' he disclosed idly. Then, with a slow, easy smile that unaccountably had her heart pounding, 'What do you think of the idea?'

Annoyed with herself for having allowed him to generate such a reaction within her, even if involuntary, Devon took her anger out on him. 'Since I won't be living here any more if it does happen, what does it matter what I think?' she snubbed before walking swiftly across the dunes and on to the gently sloping beach.

Hunt followed casually, his expression enigmatic. 'You're a real little tiger when aroused, aren't you, sweetheart?' he drawled. 'However, I would recommend you to cool it somewhat or you may find yourself engendering the same feelings in others.'

'In other words, I'm to treat you deferentially while you do as you like, is that it?' she retorted even as she whirled to face him watchfully. Unsure as to his mood, but remembering his threat to carry her in that humiliating manner again, she decided it could be prudent to keep a wary eye on him. Not that it stopped her from continuing on a scornfully gibing note. 'So what are you going to do if I fail to comply? Take my home away from me? You probably will anyway!' She glared at him direfully.

'That's as may be,' he granted with another hunching of his powerful shoulders. 'But until then I could just be tempted to settle for silencing you . . . the most effective way possible.'

'Oh, and what way would that be?' she just had time to challenge haughtily before finding out all too swiftly as he abruptly pulled her towards him and set his mouth to hers before she could think of protesting, let alone evade him.

With a smothered gasp Devon immediately hit out at him, only to have her arms pinioned against her sides when his own enfolding arms swept her closer. Frantic now lest the lips that were moving against hers so demandingly somehow managed to induce a response as they had the afternoon before, she tried holding her soft mouth rigid, but to no avail she discovered in despair, as it seemed determined to disregard her efforts at control and traitorously parted in submission.

Again he had succeeded in catching her off-guard, but that was little consolation when she was all too confusedly and embarrassedly aware that her lips were beginning to cling to his with an ardour she had never before experienced, even with her fiancé.

When Hunt finally raised his head, temporarily Devon could only stare at him helplessly until she had regained some of her composure and then she broke free infuriatedly. 'When I tell my father about this . . .!' she threatened on a ragged and resentful note.

His lips twisted wryly. 'That I kissed you—or that you responded . . . again?' he taunted.

'I—you . . . that has nothing to do with it!' she was reduced to contending uncomfortably, her embarrassment complete at knowing full well there was no way she could actually refute such a claim. 'How—how dare you keep a-assaulting me in such a fashion! I happen to be engaged, and—and I would appreciate it if you'd respect that fact!'

'Because your fiancé would object?'

'Because *I* object!' she all but shouted.

'Although only afterwards, hmm?'

Devon flushed hotly. 'No! I. . . . Oh, you're the most despicable man it's ever been my misfortune to know!' she denounced, and turning away, began walking along the beach with her head downbent.

And that was the whole trouble, she deliberated half angrily, half defeatedly. As he had so correctly surmised, apart from her father and Garth, she *didn't* know many other men, at least not well, and where Hunt was concerned that inexperience really had her at a loss as to how to deal with him. He was totally different from anyone she had ever met and he made her feel perturbingly vulnerable on occasion, particularly when he utilised that pointed mockery of his with such telling effect.

'You know, if you keep heading off on your own like this you'll have me thinking my presence is unwanted.' A wryly amused voice suddenly sounded beside her.

Devon half shrugged, but didn't speak, despite the great temptation to do so. It was really too soon for her to want to engage in another confrontation, verbal or otherwise, especially since the last one had been so disastrous from her standpoint.

'Nor was it my intention to silence you completely for the remainder of the morning,' Hunt went on in the same humorous accents.

Starting to smoulder inwardly once more—he really was the most unsettling and aggravating individual she had ever come across!—it was impossible for her to continuing holding her tongue while he enjoyed himself at her expense.

'And it was my understanding this tour was to enable you to see something of the island, not simply to provide you with the opportunity to continually bait me!' she snapped.

'You were the one who began by playing cute, beautiful,' he drawled succinctly.

Unfortunately, that that was another claim she couldn't in all honesty repudiate didn't make Devon feel any better. The more so when she suspected that no matter how she had behaved it wouldn't have precluded that goading attitude of his from coming to the fore.

'Oh, for heaven's sake, stop calling me that!' she directed irritably instead, hopeful of diverting him. It was easier than trying to defend the indefensible.

'Calling you what . . . beautiful?' he quizzed lazily, his eyes roaming over her perfectly formed features and slender, curving shape thoroughly, and bringing a warm wave of colour to her cheeks as a result. 'But you are . . . very! Or hasn't your fiancé ever told you that?'

Actually, he hadn't, but she had no intention of admitting as much. Besides, her Aunt Violet always maintained it was what was on the inside that counted, not the outside, and she said as much to the man beside her.

'Well, I've still always believed in saying what I think, and I don't intend to stop now,' she was informed in leisurely but decisive tones. Suddenly, he laughed. 'No matter if you do apparently find it disconcerting.'

So he'd guessed that, had he? she fumed. All the more reason probably why he continued to do it! 'Unwelcome, is how I would have put it,' she consequently parried in a sardonic voice. And hurriedly seeking a less personal subject, waved her arm to indicate the view to seaward. 'Well, now that you're here, does it meet with your approval?' her enquiry was facetiously made. With the tide almost to its lowest ebb, it was really one of the least prepossessing areas of the island. Only the small patch of mosquito-infested mangroves with its tangled root systems and thick, oozing mud was worse, and that was next on her itinerary for his inspection!

Briefly, Hunt's gaze took in the gnarled ti-trees lining the dunes, their twisted limbs evidence of the force of the winds that could sweep in from the open ocean, and then moved on to the low, undulating ridges of shell-encrusted beach rock that stretched unbroken from high water mark to fifty yards or more out to sea. In this section there was no coral visible at all.

'Not particularly,' he owned at length, giving Devon cause for a surreptitious smile of satisfaction. 'But then I imagine it wasn't supposed to either.'

With her smile fading even more rapidly than it had appeared—her father couldn't possibly have deduced her intentions and warned him accordingly, could he?—she rounded her aquamarine eyes in an expression of innocent surprise. 'Whatever do you mean? How should I know what appeals to you? I'm merely showing you the island ... as asked, that's all.' Her curling lashes lowered a little, her glance becoming taunting. 'Or were you anticipating total perfection?'

'Uh-uh.' He shook his head slowly. 'I've done enough research on the subject to have a fair idea of what I'd find.' Pausing, he added drily. 'As well as harbouring an extremely strong suspicion you wouldn't be revealing Cowrie's best features willingly.'

Devon impulsively gave a disgruntled grimace. He always seemed to be one step ahead of her! Or was she just transparent? Either way it didn't exactly fill her with confidence at being able to circumvent *his* plans.

'We had to start somewhere,' she offered in pseudo deprecation.

'Mmm, so we did,' he smiled easily. In fact, he always had a ready smile, and a far too damned attractive one at that, observed Devon irrelevantly, and much to her vexation as well as consternation. 'Then while we're here we might as well view it in close-up, mightn't we?' Lifting a hand to the nape of her neck he began urging her along with him towards the undulating rock, catching her completely by surprise in realising he was even interested in looking at it more closely. Garth really hadn't been.

Treading carefully as they went in order to avoid the sharp-edged shells that were fixed to the rocks in patches, they made their way out some distance from the shore to where the sandy pools between the ridges were a little deeper, and then proceeded to walk slowly in a line parallel to the beach. Most of the crystal-clear pockets of water contained some forms of life—crabs, small fish, and the like—but it was the occupants of some of the larger ones that had them stopping. A few were temporarily playing host to some young stingarees and manta rays, while at the bottom of others basked some small, beautifully marked epaulette sharks.

'We get quite a number of those,' advised Devon in what she trusted was a suitably warning tone, even though the species was actually harmless. With her home at stake, she'd decided this was to be a no holds barred war and meant to make use of anything and everything she possibly could.

'It's just as well they don't trouble humans, then, isn't it?' Hunt countered with a wryly knowing grin that immediately told her that effort had been unsuccessful. 'How about the other, less inoffensive, kinds?'

'Oh, we see loads of them too,' she exaggerated airily, trying again. 'Black tips, white tips, tigers, whalers, hammerheads. We often find them trapped in the lagoon after the tide's turned and the water's too low for them to get out again over the reef.'

'Often?' A dark brow peaked meaningfully.

'Well, occasionally,' she was prepared to concede, shrugging. More in the order of perhaps one or two a year if the truth were known, but she wasn't about to tell him that.

'Nor do all these species you mentioned happen to be dangerous, do they?'

'Oh, I don't know about that,' she evaded.

'I do,' he returned, expressively dry.

Devon attempted to camouflage her frustration as best she was able. Blast the man! He *did* appear to have done his homework, as her father had claimed. 'Yes—well—I guess it all—er—depends on which book you read on the subject,' she made an effort to pass the matter off with as much nonchalance as she could muster.

Hunt didn't even bother to reply, and not because he was in the process of divesting himself of his T-shirt and draping it around the back of his neck either, she suspected, but simply because his silence showed more adequately than words would have done just what he thought of her explanation. Deciding two defeats were enough, she began heading back to the beach with the surefootedness of long practise.

For a time Hunt continued on their original course, but when the rock began to peter out he too made his way back to shore, and only a little less agilely than she had done, she noted with some asperity. Wasn't there anything he failed at? The only time Garth had been out there with her it had taken him an age to gingerly return to the sand.

'So what's the next delight you doubtlessly have in store for me?' Hunt questioned whimsically on rejoining her.

In the act of studiously trying to ignore the imposing sight he made as the skin of his muscled torso gleamed like burnished mahogany beneath the sun's brilliant rays—good lord, she wasn't an adolescent to be affected so by mere physical attributes, was she? Devon rushed into unthinking speech.

'The mangroves,' she blurted, and then promptly berated herself for having been so informative. She had intended keeping them as a surprise.

'That should be fun,' he drawled on a satirical note. 'Maybe we'll see a few large mud crabs on our way through.'

From having been pleasurably anticipating his aversion at discovering them, it was Devon who now looked aghast. 'I'm not going in there!' she expostulated, pointing to the dense green-leaved mass that suddenly seemed all too close. 'And especially not in bare feet! You have to scramble up and over all their roots—when you're not sinking up to your knees in slimy mud, that is—and besides, the mosquitoes are big enough and ferocious enough to carry you off bodily ... and all while they're systematically draining your full blood supply, of course!'

He merely shrugged imperturbably. 'It was your idea to bring me here.'

'Only in order to show you, not to give you a tree by tree inspection!'

'Well, while I'm having a look around we may as well do it thoroughly.'

Almost to the edge of the area now, Devon really began to hang back in earnest. 'You can if you like, but I'm definitely not!' she declared flatly.

'Oh, yes you are,' he insisted, and abruptly linking his fingers with hers, made certain she could only lag so far behind. 'You're my guide, remember?'

'Not for clambering through mangrove swamps I'm not!' she defied, desperately but futilely attempting to jerk free as she felt the sand beneath her feet already becoming overlaid with a fine film of silt. Then, when he displayed no sign of relenting and she began sinking a trifle deeper, 'Hunt! Please! Okay, I apologise for having brought you along here, but please don't make me go in there. It's dark and creepy, and messy, and I hate it!'

Pausing at last, Hunt turned to eye her measuringly. 'For once, I think you might be telling the truth.'

Devon averted her gaze guiltily, but elected to side-step the issue by querying urgently, pleadingly, 'You're not really going to make me go in there, are you?'

'Well, I guess that all depends on just what you intend to replace it with, doesn't it?' he proposed indolently, but no less implicitly for all that.

'The—the rock pool,' she offered hopefully, even though that was another of the island's features she had meant to conveniently by-pass, but at the moment too relieved at being given an opportunity to avoid the mangroves to really object to such an obvious form of blackmail. Or the fact that he still had hold of her hand.

'Whereabouts is that?'

She waved her free hand vaguely in the direction of a small hill they had just passed. 'A—a little way up there.'

'Something you forgot to mention before, hmm?' sardonically.

Devon flushed. 'I—umm—thought you could see that some—some other time.'

The fingers laced with hers tightened their grip imperceptibly. 'Some other time after I'd decided the place wasn't worth buying after all, no doubt,' he surmised.

Exactly! Although she could hardly admit as much. 'Dad probably would have told you about it anyway,' she shrugged defensively. 'It's formed by the natural spring that provides most of our fresh water.' She stopped, her expression a mixture of defiance and diffidence. 'Well, are we going to—to see it or not?'

He suddenly uttered a light laugh, his deep blue eyes crinkling with amusement. 'Anything would be preferable to mangroves, wouldn't it?'

When coupled with her own thankfulness, his good humour had Devon smiling involuntarily in response. 'I can vouch for that,' she confirmed on a fervent note.

'Besides, I had no intention of going through there, in any case,' he disclosed with a provoking grin as they began retracing their steps. 'I've been in mangroves before and unless one's on a research trip I wouldn't exactly call it a pleasurable experience.'

'Oh, you heel!' Her smile was swiftly replaced with a simmering glare. And to think he'd had her pleading with him not to carry out his threat! 'You deliberately made me believe. . .' Too indignant to continue she now concentrated all her efforts into trying to wrench her hand from his instead.

'Successfully, too, it would appear,' he wasn't above rubbing it in. 'And you can forget about that,' watching her futile attempts to prise herself loose with a patent amusement that nettled her even more, 'because I've decided I like the arrangement. I know exactly where you are and what you're up to this way.'

'Well, isn't that just great for you!' she gibed rancorously. 'However, I *don't* happen to like it!'

'Tough!' he retorted, drily impervious. 'Perhaps you should have been less perverse and un-cooperative.'

Devon's breathing quickened uncontrollably. With someone as arrogant and uncaring of decency as he was, she doubted his attitude would have been any different no matter how helpful she'd been. Moreover, if such a thing were possible, it may even have been worse!

'Well, I wasn't, and I don't intend to be in future either,' she flared rebelliously.

The solid muscles of his back, clearly visible from her determinedly lagging position, rippled smoothly beneath his bronzed skin as his shoulders lifted in a gesture of total unconcern. 'Then our time together could prove extremely discomfiting . . . at least for one of us,' he turned to counsel in mocking tones.

He was meaning for her, of course, seethed Devon, and sent him a fulminating glare in return. He'd done nothing but arbitrarily ride roughshod over her wishes ever since his arrival, but she was damned if he was going to get everything his own way! If it was the last thing she did, she would ensure he received his come-uppance for some of those defeats, somehow! she vowed vehemently.

# CHAPTER FOUR

THE rock pool had always seemed a magical place to Devon with its glittering, cascading waterfall and richly tropical surrounds, and where the sparkling water was always refreshingly cool even on the hottest day. As she followed Hunt to its boulder-strewn edge on this occasion, though, she immediately saw that the waterfall wasn't flowing—a sure indication that her father must have been in the midst of refilling the water tanks at the house from a smaller pool located a little further up the slope—and promptly experienced a sense of satisfaction knowing that its loss detracted considerably from the area's charm.

'You look inordinately pleased about something all of a sudden,' Hunt surprised her by abruptly remarking. Hell, she couldn't possibly have been so unthinking as to allow her gratification to show outwardly, could she? she despaired. 'I don't suppose there could be something missing, could there?' His eyes narrowed as they surveyed the pool alertly.

Devon only just managed to suppress an incredulous gasp. Not even he could be that astute, surely! 'L-like what?' her disbelief had her attempt at feigned innocence being voiced in a stammer.

'A waterfall, maybe,' he managed to shock her even further by hazarding. 'That rock face on the far side didn't get that smoothly worn appearance from nothing, and besides . . .' he paused, his lips curving wryly, 'Royce was telling me that Matt had said there was one when he was enquiring about the island's water supply yesterday.'

If her parent had been present, Devon could have hit him as well as the man beside her, for not only having provided the information in the first place but for thereby also putting Hunt in a position where he could both goad and defeat her with the knowledge at the same time.

'Oh, that,' she now had no choice but to pretend to recall, albeit in a somewhat testy fashion. 'Funny, I didn't even realise it was missing.'

'Hilarious,' he quipped. His eyes filled with lazy taunting. 'Victory number one to me, huh?'

Devon controlled her escalating emotions with difficulty, and it was only by clenching her free hand at her side that she did refrain from lashing out at him physically. 'Has anyone ever told you just what a hateful, callous and unbearable animal you really are, Hunter Kincaid?' she lashed scathingly with her tongue in lieu.

'No, can't say they have.' His indiffferent reply was accompanied by an equally negligent shrug. 'Why, has someone told you just what a selfish, intractable, and thoroughly wayward little jade you are?'

The very quietness with which he delivered his stricture, as much as the unexpectedness of it, had her biting at her lip doubtfully and her anger suddenly disappearing as less positive thoughts rushed to take its place. He was the only person to have ever accused her of having such faults, and the knowledge that this morning she had unquestionably displayed every one of them made her feel slightly ashamed.

Not that she cared what Hunt thought of her, of course, but she was well aware just how disappointed her father would be in her if he ever came to hear of it, and that she didn't want at any cost. The alternative, though—abiding by his wishes and showing Hunt everything Cowrie did have to offer—would require a degree of willpower on her part she wasn't sure she even possessed. Nevertheless, for her father's sake at least, it was obviously an effort she was going to have to make, she realised dismally, and with a convulsive swallow set about doing just that before what little conviction she did have deserted her.

'I'm sorry,' she apologised miserably, not quite looking at him. 'As you said, it—it's Dad's decision to make, not mine.' Swallowing again, she made herself divulge on a falsely bright note, 'Actually, it's much prettier here when the water's flowing, and—and the rock's so smooth you can slide down it. It's good fun. Just like a slippery dip. The bottom of the pool's all sand too, and. . .'

'Devon, that's enough!' Hunt cut in on her sharply.

'No, there's more yet,' she went on in the same lively tone as if once having started it was imperative she said it all. 'It shelves gently this end as well so it's quite easy for elderly people or—or children to. . .'

'*Devon!*' There was a steely ring of command in his voice when he interrupted this time, and releasing her fingers at last he cupped her head between his two hands and resolutely forced her face up to his. 'What the hell's got into you?'

'N-nothing,' she denied huskily, and blinking quickly on feeling the sting of salt under her eyelids. She wasn't going to make a fool of herself by crying in front of him—she wasn't! 'I've just decided to—to do what Dad wanted me to, that's all, and I don't s-see what you've got to complain about. It's the type of—of information you wanted, isn't it?'

'But not relayed in this manner, for God's sake!'

'Oh, I didn't realise there was a particular way it had to be delivered,' she gibed tremulously. 'I thought getting what you wanted was all you cared about.'

'Then you got it all wrong, didn't you?' he smiled gently, his voice resuming its customary drawling inflection. 'Because all I ever wanted from you was a little reasonable co-operation.' Then, with a disarming widening of his shapely mouth, 'Plus maybe a smile or two.'

Devon licked at her lips distractedly, her mind in a whirl. Until yesterday her life had been calm and uncomplicated, but since his arrival all that had changed, drastically, so that she now felt as if everything familiar to her was being inexorably swept away—including her control over her own emotions—for instead of concentrating on the threat he indisputably presented to her way of life, her senses now only seemed capable of registering an overwhelming and wholly disconcerting awareness in response to that attractive curving of his firmly moulded mouth. A reaction she found so perturbing that it at least had the relieving effect of banishing any likelihood of tears as she fought frantically to overcome it.

'Yes—well—then if you've seen all you want to here, I think it's time we were getting back,' she proposed expressionlessly, her gaze fastened purposely to the strong column of his throat, her features studiously composed to reflect none of her inner turmoil. 'Even though Dad may have said he'd help Aunt Violet, I'd still rather not be too late.'

Momentarily, she thought he wasn't going to release

her and she trembled inwardly—the little control she was managing to portray was still very fragile and she doubted it could withstand any sort of challenge to its stability—but then he exhaled deeply and dropped his hands to his hips.

'Okay, sweetheart, I guess we've gone about as far as we can go this morning, haven't we?' he declared on a vaguely rueful note.

Too far, from Devon's point of view, although she found it somewhat enigmatic that he apparently thought so as well. After all, he'd achieved what *he* wanted. Not that she intended puzzling over it, though. She was only too pleased to know she would soon be free of his disturbing presence, and with that consoling thought in mind she made for the path that led back to the house with eager steps.

'So why wasn't the water flowing?' Hunt broke in on her reverie unexpectedly, causing her to start.

'Oh—er—because Dad's pumping it out from another pool closer to its source, I expect,' she disclosed, grudgingly. In spite of her decision not to go against her father's wishes, it still came hard to actually go along with them.

'You mean, the spring's flow is that weak?' he frowned.

Tempted to endorse his assumption for a second, her shoulders suddenly slumped resignedly. What was the use? Her father would probably only put him wise to the truth of the matter in due course. 'Usually only around this time of the year . . . before the onset of the wet,' she advised finally.

'Has it ever dried up altogether?' His probing became more intent.

'Only once, I believe, a long time ago when the rains

really didn't fall at all in any quantity,' she sighed. She
would dearly have loved to have said it occurred all
the time.

'So what happened?'

'Water was shipped in from the mainland,' she
shrugged. 'We sometimes have to do that now during
the summer, in any case, if our consumption goes too
high. There's no hassle about it—it's just extremely
expensive.'

He nodded thoughtfully. 'You've never considered
increasing your rain storage capacity?'

Devon pressed her lips together vexedly. 'Yes,
Dad's thought about it, but in comparison to the
number of times it's necessary to ship water in, the
cost of constructing additional tanks out here is even
more exorbitant!' Pausing, she cast him a meaningful
sidelong glance from beneath long lashes. 'Naturally,
if the number of guests and staff on the island was
increased more tanks would be an absolute necessity,
as would larger generators in order to provide
sufficient light and power.'

'Don't worry, that thought had occurred to me,' he
owned wryly, and thereby gave her spirits a much
needed lift as she wondered if that wasn't the line she
should have taken all along. If he believed the costs
involved in developing the island to the standard he
envisaged to be too high, he wasn't likely to go ahead
with the project, was he?'

Consequently, as they presently neared the house,
she deliberately took him past the maintenance area so
he might see for himself just how much of the
equipment would need to be replaced or upgraded to
enable the island to cater for a larger population, and
for the first time was pleased to note how obvious it

was that even the buildings housing the machinery badly required extensive repairs. In fact, to provide adequate protection for new equipment they would undoubtedly have to be replaced in their entirety, and with the law these days insisting all new constructions be cyclone proof, the expense of so doing could be expected to rise by as much as another third, she reasoned with unqualified satisfaction.

'I'm beginning to see now why the idea of selling appeals to Matt. That equipment's sure only got a limited life,' was Hunt's sole comment as he also viewed the area with assessing eyes, but it was sufficient to have some of Devon's pleasure fading a little.

She hadn't really considered it in that light. If the generators did break down permanently, which was quite a possibility considering they had been doing so temporarily with increasing frequency during the last few years, just where would the money come from to repair, or worse still, purchase substitutes for them? With no intention of permitting her companion to guess at the doubts he had unwittingly raised within her, however, she simply hunched a golden shoulder impassively.

'Oh, I wouldn't exactly say that,' she disagreed. 'They used to build them to last in the old days, you know, and these have been going strong for years.'

'My point entirely . . . too many years!' he had no compunction in emphasising significantly.

'Then maybe you should reconsider your ideas for purchasing the place!' she was stung into suggesting.

'Uh-uh!' he discounted that notion lazily, and dashed her rising hopes as a result. 'There's still a long way to go yet before I'm likely to do that.'

'How long?' she grimaced.

'Hopefully we'll know for certain by the end of this
month. If it is to go ahead I'd prefer to have it all
settled before the wet begins so we can utilise those
months to have the plans, plus all the other necessary
arrangements finalised, and then we should be in a
position to begin work immediately the rains have
finished.'

Time being of the essence because time was also
money, she presumed, pulling another disgruntled
face. Her thoughts raced on searching for other
difficulties. 'And the local authorities? What if you
should buy it and then they reject your application for
development?'

'We've already had discussions with them to explain
our iddeas, and provided we don't deviate from them
they can see no reason for it not being approved.'

More was the pity! She began racking her brain
once more. 'Well, what about an—an architect, then?
You surely can't mean to have plans drawn without
one at least having visited the island?'

At the house now, Hunt leant casually against the
bottom post of the back steps. 'He'll be arriving next
week, as a matter of fact. Along with a couple of
surveyors, our construction foreman, and a few others
whose job it is to see that nothing's been forgotten and
that it all goes without a hitch,' he informed her drily.

'You've got it all down pat, haven't you?' she
heaved. Followed by a distinctly more enthusiastic,
'Although once they arrive, I suppose there'll be no
need for you to remain here, will there?'

'Sorry,' he grinned and tapped her provokingly
under the chin, 'but having discovered the company to
be so congenial here, I've decided to turn it into a

working vacation and, therefore, don't expect to be leaving until the last of my staff does.'

Devon sighed disconsolately and mounted the first step. So there was to be no relief there either! She half swung towards him, her turquoise eyes troubled as they connected with his. 'And if—if you did buy it, when would we have to—to leave?' Her voice shook in spite of her attempts to keep it steady.

Hunt dragged a hand through his hair roughly, tousling it, and then with a heavily expelled breath trailed his fingers across her cheek softly. 'Don't worry about it, sweetheart,' he urged on a deeper, more vibrant note than usual. 'We'll work something out . . . if and when the time comes.'

With the briefest of nods she hurried up the remaining steps and on to the verandah. Just by his actions he had made it clear it wouldn't be long afterwards, she surmised.

'I'll see you again this afternoon, shall I?' His voice reached up to her from the ground where he was in line with her as he began heading for the bottom camp.

Stopping, she looked down at him with a frown drawing her winged brows together. 'To continue our tour, you mean?'

'Uh-huh!'

'Oh, but I can't this afternoon,' she was pleased to be able to inform him, and it did much to lighten her mood. 'I have to help Dad load the trailer with whatever needs to go back on the launch, and then reload it again with the incoming stores.'

'Wouldn't it be more appropriate if your fiancé did that?'

'Not really.' She shook her head slightly. 'He

doesn't work here yet, he's only a visitor at the moment, just like you. The difference being, *he* isn't as abrasive as you are, thankfully!' she mocked dulcetly.

His ensuing grin was anything but remorseful, although it was totally devastating from Devon's standpoint, as her suddenly racing pulse could verify. 'And are you also thankful he evidently doesn't kiss you as often either?' he dared to taunt in return.

Devon's cheeks flamed as she gasped and looked about her anxiously. It would be even more embarrassing if anyone had overheard his comment, and that he had made it at all . . . well, that just proved how correct her thoughts about him had been.

'Yes, I am!' she threw back at him stormily. Then, realising what she could be implying—as no doubt he had been! 'No! Of course not!' And when that didn't sound right either, 'I mean, there's no evidence about . . . oh, why don't you just go away and leave me alone!' she concluded on a fractious note. The more she said, the more she only seemed to play into his hands.

'When you tell me when our little tour is to continue, maybe I will,' he offered chafingly.

'Oh, in the morning, I suppose,' she retorted flusteredly. Any time, as long as it prevented him from making any other such mortifying remarks and he left right now!

'I'll see you after breakfast, then?'

'Yes—yes,' she acceded swiftly and made good her departure before he could utter another word.

As he had apparently promised, her father was helping his sister in the kitchen when Devon entered and his bushy brows promptly lifted in an unspoken query. When she didn't immediately reply, however, but walked across to the sink to begin washing her hands, he was forced into making it a verbal one.

'Well, how did it go?' he quizzed wryly.

'Oh, super! I can't remember the last time I had such an—umm—invigorating morning!' she alleged with just enough sarcasm for her own ears.

'That's nice, dear,' smiled her Aunt Violet. 'Where did you go?'

'To Rocky Point, back along the beach to the mangroves, and then past the pool,' Devon relayed with a grimace through the window in front of her for the tall figure she could see heading in the direction of the camp.

'Saving the best for last, eh?' It was her father again. Drying her hands, she turned to face him and knew immediately from his shrewd expression that he was fully aware she hadn't intended anything of the kind, and that he had also picked up her earlier caustic intonation.

'Something like that, I guess,' she shrugged uncomfortably.

His eyes were unwavering as they held hers. 'You will be showing him everything, though?'

'Yes.' Her affirmation was given in a listless murmur. 'I've arranged to take him round the rest tomorrow morning ... even though I would have liked to have spent some time with Garth,' she added a little more spiritedly.

'Well, as it so happens, you wouldn't have been able to do that, in any event,' he half smiled sympathetically. 'You see, his father was in touch with him while you were away to say he was needed back in the office, and he's leaving on the launch this afternoon.'

His news didn't altogether come as a surprise to Devon. Garth had said as much might happen when he'd first arrived a week and a half ago, but she did find it rather demoralising that it had had to occur at a time when she needed an ally most.

To her father, though, all she said was, 'I see. Then that would appear to settle that, wouldn't it?'

'I'm sorry, love, I know how pleased you've been having him here,' he immediately consoled. 'Besides, perhaps he'll be able to make it back again on next week's launch and finish his holidays then.'

She nodded, smiling faintly. If Garth could, it would at least give her *something* to look forward to. As it was, she suspected it was going to be less and less easy to find anything to be happy about as the island became inundated with Eastern Development personnel.

Since it wasn't possible for them to discuss the matter during lunch—there were too many guests around, not to mention her father—Devon had to wait, impatiently, until the meal was concluded and she'd helped her aunt clear everything away before she and Garth had the chance to be alone, and they promptly made for the chairs on the unoccupied verandah.

'So what was your morning like?' Garth was the first to speak once they were seated.

'Even worse than I expected it would be,' she both grimaced and sighed. 'He's the most arrogant and unfeeling brute I've ever met, but even more infuriating that that, he's too damned on the ball!' She sucked in a resentful breath and added disgustedly, 'He *knew* what I was trying to do all the time!'

'Oh, well, never mind,' Garth dismissed her

complaints negligently, to her amazement. 'At least I've got good news.'

Putting aside her own feelings for the moment, she leant forward interestedly. 'You mean, Dad did have more discussions with Royce Attwood and you sat in on them too this time?'

'Mmm,' he endorsed eagerly. 'And you know, it is a tremendous deal they're offering. I doubt your father will ever get a better one.'

Devon could only stare at him in shocked disbelief, feeling as if she had just been betrayed. It was the last thing she had expected him to say, and certainly not what she wanted to hear! 'But—but I thought you intended to find fault with the idea . . . not praise it!' she charged aggrievedly on recovering.

At least he had the grace to shift a little discomfitedly, she noted. 'Yes—well—I was going to, but honestly, if I'd done so it could only have been regarded as nit-picking. What I'm trying to say is, if they keep to their word, your father's got it made, and with our share of. . .'

'What share?' she interrupted sharply. 'Cowrie belongs to Dad, no one else. There are no *shares*!'

'Not at the moment, no, but that's apparently his idea, see. For us all to share the proceeds.'

'Well, I'm not interested in any share!' she flashed. 'I'm only interested in our remaining on the island.'

'And that's just being blindly obstinate!' he retorted in irritable accents. 'Can't you understand? This would set us up for life!'

Which was all the island meant to him, was it? A ticket to an imposing life style! Her gaze unconsciously drifted down to the beach below the house, the sight of gently swaying palms reaching up to a brilliant blue sky, the white sand lapped by crystalline waters that shimmered and danced as the sun's rays bounced off each ripple filling her with an emotion that was hard to describe, but which always brought a smile of contentment to her lips. At least, it always had until now.

'I was under the impression we already were, just by being able to live here,' she dragged her eyes back from the beautiful scene in order to impart pensively.

Garth's mouth pulled into an exasperated line. 'Oh, come on, Devon, be realistic! You know very well the island's been going downhill for years, and it will hardly be the end of the world if you have to live somewhere else—particularly under the prevailing circumstances.'

'Oh?' Her brows arched sardonically. 'I don't remember you thinking that way when you first heard of it. In fact, you were highly indignant at the thought of not being able to manage the place, as I recall.'

He dropped his gaze, abashed, but only momentarily, and then he was looking up again to impress, 'But that was before I knew all the facts. And believe me, managing this place as it is can't even come close to competing with the opportunities that would be available if it was disposed of. I mean, have you any idea exactly how much we would actually get from such a sale?'

'No, and I've not the slightest desire to find out either!' she announced in clipped tones. 'I couldn't care less what they're offering because I'm more than content to remain right here.' She paused, her glance cynical. 'Money doesn't buy happiness, you know, Garth.'

'No?' It was his brows that leapt satirically upwards

now. 'Well, it would sure beat the hell out of the hand-to-mouth existence we'd have to endure if we tried continuing with this place!' Then, moderating his voice persuasively on seeing the hurt look that crossed her face, 'Besides, it's always been in the back of my mind that we'd sell some time in the not too distant future, anyway. You must know yourself, even if you are loath to admit it, that we couldn't retain it indefinitely, and especially with the number of guests gradually decreasing. Times have changed, Devon, and to expect to keep an island like this to yourself just isn't possible, or practical, any longer. So as far as I'm concerned the most logical alternative is to acknowledge the writing on the wall, accept gratefully a far from measly remuneration in recompense, and begin a new life elsewhere. When all's said and done,' he shrugged, 'Northport's not such a bad place and there's certainly a greater variety of things to do there.'

'Except I don't happen to want to live in Northport!' she promptly asserted stubbornly. It was the first time he had ever mentioned to her about having secretly considered parting with the island and as a result it made her wonder if he'd ever really intended to manage the guesthouse as they'd planned. That he may not have, now made her feel even more deceived, and therefore considerably less receptive, if that was possible, to his arguments.

'All right, some other town then,' he allowed obligingly. 'Where would you suggest?'

'Cowrie Island,' she said deliberately, her chin lifting. 'I told you, I'm not interested in living anywhere else.'

'And as I told you, you're just being obstinate!' He

glared at her in obvious aggravation. 'Although you're going to have to accept it some time, you know, whether you want to or not, because unless I miss my guess, your father's going to go through with this deal and there's not a thing you can do to stop it!' Halting, his expression became resolute. 'And all things considered, I say good luck to him!'

'Good luck to him ... or good luck to you?' The bitter gibe was out before she could halt it.

Notwithstanding that he glanced away temporarily, Garth slung out of his chair in a rancorous movement. 'If that's all you've got to say, I can see I'm wasting my time even discussing it with you! You've just got this fixation about the place so that you believe anyone who disagrees with you must have an ulterior motive!' he retaliated before storming off along the verandah. Almost to the front door he stopped and turned to face her again with a heaved sigh. 'I'll see you down at the jetty before I leave, okay?'

Devon nodded mechanically, her lip caught between even white teeth as she watched him pass through the doorway, her gaze both sorrowful and contemplative. No matter how much anger he had displayed at her insinuation, she was still disappointedly aware that her suspicion wasn't as wide of the mark as he would like her to believe. However, it was the thought that that was what may have been in his mind all along that really hurt. That, and his evident incomprehension as to how deeply she felt about the island.

With a sigh, she rubbed her fingers against her temple dismally. Why, even Hunter Kincaid had shown more forbearance than her fiancé had by saying he could understand why she was so reluctant to see Cowrie sold, she recollected. And it wasn't only on her own account that she wanted to see it retained either, as Garth had tried to imply! There was her father and her aunt to consider too. The former, because it would provide him with the means to go off on his sailing trip—which she just couldn't bring herself to believe was an activity he should undertake—and the latter, because she hated being idle, and without her guests to cater to Devon knew her aunt would be lost— irrespective of being wealthy!

In the background there suddenly came the sound of the island's mini-tractor approaching, signalling that her father would shortly be loading its accompanying trailer with their departing guests' luggage ready for delivery to the jetty, and Devon rose slowly to her feet, preparing to go and assist him. As she turned to leave, however, her soft lips took on a rueful curve as recollections of her distressing and disappointing dispute with her fiancé refused to be dismissed. And to think she had considered Garth her foremost ally! she grimaced expressively.

The *Coral Trader* duly arrived just before four and for a time the old wharf was a hive of activity. Since it was Devon's job to attend to all incoming guests the first thing she did was to greet their two new arrivals and by way of the tractor and now unloaded trailer, which had seats constructed along its sides for just such a purpose, transport the middle-aged couple and their baggage up to the house where they were delivered into the capable and attentive hands of her aunt. This accomplished, she then returned down the hill to help with the more demanding work of loading their incoming stores—always greater at this time of year in preparation for the cyclone season ahead when there was the possibility the weather could prevent the launch keeping to its weekly schedule.

Since those people leaving the island, except for Garth who was leaning casually against one of the jetty's bollards some short distance away from the landing steps, had already boarded the boat, the area was a little less congested when she made it back, although as the crew brought more and more boxes and crates ashore it rapidly took on an obstructed appearance again.

Also, she noted with some dissatisfaction, Hunt and another two young men she didn't know had now joined her father and were at the moment engaged in a discussion with the launch's skipper. With their last disconcerting parting still vividly in mind, Devon was even more reluctant to find herself in his vicinity now than usual and consequently brought the tractor to a halt beside the mound of stores furthest away and began stacking them into the trailer.

A few seconds later Garth ambled across to her and seated himself on a crate close by. 'I'm sorry I've had to break up our time together like this, but I'll see if I can get a ride out on a yacht coming this way—if there is one—for the weekend at least. All right?' he sounded quietly.

'Mmm, that will be good if you can,' Devon half smiled as she stopped for a moment to wipe perspiration from her forehead with her forearm, avoiding any mention of their argument. 'We could have a barbecue down on the beach—just the two of us.'

'I'd like that,' he acceded just as carefully. 'It's not often we get the chance to be really alone.'

They would have if he could only be bothered to

bestir himself a little instead of lazing about the house so often, she thought wryly, but judiciously didn't voice her thoughts aloud. 'No, well, that's one of the penalties when there's more often than not guests around, I suppose,' she allowed generously instead, resuming stacking boxes again.

He watched her in silence for a while, then suggested quietly, 'So why don't you come back with me to Northport this afternoon too? You know you're always welcome at home, and at least we'd have more to do.'

Devon ignored his last comment as she came to a halt once more. 'It's a little late to make such a decision now. The launch is almost ready to leave,' she part laughed, part grimaced wryly. 'In any case, I'm sorry but I couldn't possibly leave during the next few weeks. Not with the added work the extra visitors will make for Aunt Violet and Dad.'

'What extra visitors?' he frowned. 'I only saw two get off today to replace the half dozen leaving, and your bookings always fall off for the next couple of months, don't they?'

'Usually,' she averred, nodding. 'But this year things aren't quite the same as normal,' with an expressive sigh, 'and apparently we're about to receive an influx of Eastern Development personnel.'

'Oh! To check the place out and decide what requires doing, I suppose,' he deduced, sounding nowhere near as displeased at the prospect as she had. 'They want to get it finished before the wet begins, I expect.'

'So I believe,' she came close to snapping and returned to her work resentfully. Knowing how she felt about the matter, he could at least have displayed a little more tact by camouflaging his obvious approval!

As if sensing her feelings, Garth left his seat and moved further away to rest his folded arms on the wharf's worn railing and stare down at the water below. 'Well, even you must have anticipated something of the kind happening,' he half turned to claim in a cooler tone. 'After all, they're contemplating investing a considerable sum of money in the place, and they want to be certain it's worth it.'

Devon wrestled with a heavier carton and dropped it into the trailer from a height that made everything shake. 'To ensure they're going to be repaid with a handsome profit?' she couldn't help sniping.

'Why not?' he promptly countered, his lips thinning. 'That's what makes the world go round. All losses do is create higher unemployment, and I can't imagine anyone in their right mind wanting that!'

Implying, she *wasn't* in her right mind because she objected to having her home taken over, she surmised with an angry glare as he moved further along the rail. With her indignation rising, she began grappling with a carton of tinned fruit she would normally have waited for her father to help with, only to utter a gasp of shock when a muscular arm suddenly wrapped itself about her midriff and lifted her bodily out of the way.

'What the hell do you think you're doing? That's far too heavy for you,' an all too familiar, and unwelcome, voice bit out censoriously.

Already in something of a less than submissive mood, Devon's stormy gaze passed over the darkly suntanned chest confronting her to lock defiantly with Hunt's vivid blue eyes. 'And if I don't give Dad a hand with the stores, who would you suggest does . . . Aunt Violet?' she gibed sarcastically.

'So what's wrong with hero back there?' He

gestured contemptuously over his shoulder with his thumb. 'Or is he as incompetent in shifting stores as he obviously is as a lover?'

Temporarily, Devon didn't know where to look as her cheeks burned with a self-conscious heat. She had never encountered such disturbing directness before, particularly on a personal level, and that he should continually make such remarks about her fiancé she found not only annoying and embarrassing, but extremely unsettling as well.

'No,' she finally managed to disclaim, albeit not as forcefully as she would have liked. 'It just happens that he's going back on the launch, that's all.'

With a scornful glance to where Garth was still leaning against the rail, he raised a sardonic brow. 'And it was just out of the question that he might conceivably give you a hand before he left, was it?'

'He—he's not dressed for it,' she excused with a shrug, gazing towards her fiancé herself now and noting his perfectly pressed pale grey trousers and creaseless blue shirt.

'Is he ever?' It was really more of a derisive statement than a question.

A trace of wariness darkened her eyes. 'I don't know what you mean.'

'I mean, I'd be surprised to learn he ever helped with the unloading . . . no matter how he was dressed!'

Now that she actually thought about it, Devon abruptly realised he wasn't wrong and that so used was she to there only being her father and herself to do all the work that she hadn't missed Garth's presence when he had been available to help. And perhaps that was also what her father had been referring to when he'd said only the night before that he feared Garth might not pull his weight if and when he should take over managing the island, the disquieting thought suddenly followed. It was a perturbing notion to say the least, but as there was no way she was going to disclose anything of the kind to the man before her she simply forced a look of suitably demurring amusement on to her face.

'Oh, naturally he. . . .' She broke off as her fiancé chose that moment to glance in her direction, but on seeing who was standing next to her made no move to join them, merely raising his hand in a minimal salute and heading towards the boarding ramp before she could even lift her own arm more than a few inches in response.

'Well, well, that would have to be about the most touching farewell I've ever witnessed,' Hunt immediately mocked. 'Are your reunions equally as passionate, I wonder?'

'Oh, go to hell!' Devon blazed, her eyes following Garth doubtfully. Obviously his acceptance of the scheme to buy the island still didn't extend to the man behind it. 'Not that it's any of your business, but there's a—a reason for this.'

'Had a fight over his sudden change of heart, did you?' And scathingly, in response to the astonishment that had her forgetting all about her fiancé for the moment and wondering instead how on earth he could have guessed, 'Royce told me how his eyes had lit up like the candles on a Christmas tree when he discovered how much he could stand to gain if the deal went through.'

In view of Garth's later behaviour, Devon didn't really feel in aposition to gainsay his accusation, but at the same time she didn't intend to blindly accept it either. 'Then *if* that was the case,' she stressed significantly, 'I'm surprised you're not thinking of him more favourably. After all, that just means there's one less for you to convince, doesn't it?'

'Except for one small detail,' he disputed on a taunting note. 'At present I rather think it's Matt wanting to convince *me* to buy the place.'

She bit at her lip sharply. 'Of—of course. How stupid of m-me to think otherwise,' she granted on a faltering note no amount of effort appeared capable of making steady, and pushing past him reached for the carton she had been struggling with before he interrupted her.

'And how stupid of you to think I've changed my mind about you lifting those!' Hunt retorted roughly as he once again swept her off her feet and dumped her down a few feet away. 'So why don't you just go and give that useless bastard of yours another of those incredibly fervent waves and let me do this instead, huh?'

'No! And don't you dare call him that either!' she stormed, her temper flaring ungovernably at his high-handedness and his derogatory comments as she purposely took a step forward towards the pile. 'I always help Dad with the loading and. . .'

'Well, this time you can take a rest, can't you?' An unyielding hand on her shoulder propelled her back to where she had been. 'Because if you don't,' he went on with a smile, but managing to convey a sense of menace nonetheless, 'you'll finish by wishing you had, I can assure you!'

Devon seethed impotently, aware that his sheer unpredictability made it imprudent for her to force the issue any further, and with her eyes flashing infuritatedly she flounced across to the rail to watch the launch reverse away from the jetty. Shortly, it was heading out through the reef and on its way back to Northport—Cowrie being the last island it put in at—and with a sigh she swung round to observe Hunt as he transferred the heavy cartons from the wharf to the trailer with a speed and ease she knew she could never have duplicated.

He worked with a rhythm that had his muscles flexing and relaxing in an almost continuous play of movement that, to her alarm, Devon abruptly realised she was finding fascinating, and she snatched her eyes away to concentrate on her father instead. He was still further along the jetty and similarly engaged, along with the two young men she had noticed earlier, in loading another trailer he had brought down prior to the boat's arrival. After a moment or two her curiosity began to get the better of her and she glanced back at Hunt quizzically.

'Just who are those two men assisting Dad? I don't remember seeing them before.'

'No, that's Alister and Vince. They're two of the crew from the *Kanandah*,' he relayed without looking up. Then stopping altogether, he sent her a bantering grin. 'Since there was obviously only going to be you and Matt doing the work we decided we couldn't allow one of the fair sex to do any such thing. Chauvinistic of us, wasn't it?' His lips twitched crookedly.

Under other circumstances she probably would have called it gentlemanly, but as it was. . . . 'The way you arrogantly take over, yes it is!' she concurred pungently. 'And what's more, you're filling the trailer too full. The tractor will never pull it all up the hill.' It was her turn to smile now, smugly.

In a matter of seconds he removed four of the heaviest boxes. 'How's that, then?'

'Better,' she allowed primly.

'Then we might as well get it up to the house, mightn't we?' He began striding towards the tractor.

Devon rushed forward to intercept him. 'I can at least drive that!' she protested. Followed by a wry, 'Besides, it has idiosyncrasies it just loves to demonstrate on the unknowing.'

'Okay, sweetheart, I guess that's allowable,' he conceded in an amused drawl, and while she slid behind the wheel, he perched himself on the front of the trailer.

By the time they were half way up the hill, however, Devon was beginning to wish she'd let him do the driving after all, for as he leant forward with his arms resting across his knees, his head was just about in line with her shoulder and she found the experience to be both disturbing and distracting. It was only by constantly telling herself to concentrate that she managed to get them to the house without having permitted him to disconcert her to the extent where she made some unthinking mistake whereby the tractor got the better of her.

No sooner had they pulled up alongside the back verandah than Hunt had effortlessly swung two of the large cartons into his arms and strode into the kitchen with them. Devon followed with two smaller parcels. Not even he could object to her carrying those, surely! As it happened Violet was in the room when they entered, and from her somewhat startled expression evidently surprised to see just who had arrived with her niece.

'Come on, Aunt Vi, there's a lot more where these came from. Where do you want 'em?' Hunt promptly grinned teasingly at the older woman.

Behind him, Devon waited expectantly, pleasurably, for the explosion. No one, but *no one*, called her relative Vi, and as for the Aunt ... well, considering theirs was such a short acquaintance, and he certainly wasn't any relative, anyway, she could hardly restrain a smile at the thought of him being well and truly cut down to size for once!

When Violet did reply, though, it was to leave her niece open mouthed with shock to hear her aunt chuckle in genial tones, 'You young rogue!' And pointing to the door of the storeroom near the dresser, 'In there on the right, if you would be so kind, please, Hunter.'

'Hunt,' he amended with another smile as he passed her, and once more to Devon's amazement her normally so formal aunt cheerfully complied.

When he emerged from the storeroom, Devon still hadn't moved, and her aunt frowned at her anxiously. 'Are you feeling all right, dear?' she enquired. 'You look quite strange.'

'What? Oh, yes, I'm fine, thanks, Aunt Violet,' she recovered enough to claim weakly. 'I was just—just daydreaming, that's all.' And trying to figure out just what it was about Hunter Kincaid that, to her own unbounded exasperation, had her only relations treating him as if he was one of the family and could do no wrong!

'I expect you're missing Garth already, are you?' Violet hazarded compassionately.

'More than likely,' put in Hunt uninvited and straight-faced, although the sideways glance he directed at Devon was purely goading. 'You could tell just by their tender farewells on the jetty how loath they were to part.'

Violet made a clicking sound of understanding. 'Oh, that's nice,' she smiled, all unaware of the currents that were flashing between the other two occupants of the room.

'Yes—well—it's time we were getting on, isn't it?' Devon cast the man beside her a murderous glare. 'As you said, there's a lot more to be unloaded yet. So if you've quite finished discussing me, perhaps we could finish it!' She thumped her own two parcels on to the table now and, turning round, headed for the door.

'Devon! That wasn't very polite when Hunt's obviously been good enough to offer his help,' she heard her aunt chide disappointedly, but determined she wasn't going to be pressured into apologising, she just kept walking.

'Don't worry about it, Aunt Vi, she's probably just out of sorts because her fiancé's left,' Hunt's whimsically worded excuse that followed certainly brought about a reaction, though. It had her waiting for him by the trailer with her hands clenched and her emotions simmering.

'If you don't cut out those smart remarks concerning Garth and myself, Hunter Kincaid, this time I'm assuring *you* that you'll wish you had!' she threatened irately as soon as he was within hearing distance.

'Oh?' A dark brow quirked chafingly high. 'And just how do you propose to do that, beautiful? By complaining to your father ... or even by exacting physical retribution, perhaps?'

'It could just be both!' she retaliated in as direful a

tone as she could exhibit as she swung herself on to the tractor's seat in a furious movement. His obviously mirthful unconcern rankled unbearably, the more so when she suspected that neither course of action would be likely to have the desired effect and, consequently, made any threat she could utter an empty one—of which he was as aware as she was! Without waiting to see if he was aboard, she thrust the tractor into gear and started down the hill again at a speed that, although not recommended, at least helped to release some of her turbulent emotions.

In all, they needed to make another three trips before the jetty was eventually cleared, and no one was more thankful than Devon when the last of the goods had been put away and she could finally anticipate some relief from Hunt's riling presence. That was, until her aunt apparently decided his assistance deserved some repayment apart from just a verbal one and invited him to join them for dinner, whereupon her pleasure was rapidly replaced by a sinking feeling of despair on hearing him accept.

# CHAPTER FIVE

As was customary, the island's guests and their hosts shared the same large table in the dining room for their meal that evening and, on this occasion particularly, Devon was extremely pleased that they did. It provided her with the opportunity to maintain a running conversation with them and thereby ignore the man seated next to her father on the opposite side of the table.

However, in spite of her attempts to disregard him entirely, she still wasn't able to completely subdue her curiosity as to what he and her father were discussing so earnestly, although she wasn't altogether surprised when the snatches of conversation she did manage to pick up proved to be about sailing. It had always been a great love of her father's and from what she could gather Hunt was no novice at the sport either.

What did give her cause for annoyance and concern a while later, though, was to overhear them talking about her father's long-planned sailing trip—with Hunt evidently encouraging him to go ahead with it! Reluctantly, because it was neither the time nor the place for her to be voicing her objections to the scheme, she was forced to bide her time as patiently as possible until the meal was concluded before informing Hunt in no uncertain terms to keep his unwanted comments to himself regarding her family's private affairs.

As it so happened, in fact, she even had to wait

considerably longer than that, because immediately on leaving the dining room both men disappeared into the small office at the front of the house and as her censure was really meant for the younger of the two, once again she had to defer her intentions until she could catch him on his own. It would doubtlessly be self-defeating if she made her feelings known in her father's hearing, especially now that he had some support, and from someone who—although for the life of her she couldn't understand why!—he appeared to regard so favourably.

In the end, it was nearly eleven before Hunt finally took his departure and, after making sure her father had returned inside once he'd seen his companion off, Devon hurried down the back steps and chased after her quarry determinedly.

'Hunt!' she called imperiously on almost catching up to him. 'I want to talk to you!'

He turned to face her slowly, his expression as readily provoking as always. 'Do you now,' he drawled wryly. 'That's a change. So what have I done wrong by your island to cause such a precedent this time, hmm?'

'As a matter of fact, it has nothing to do with the island,' she answered stiffly. 'It's more important than that.'

He gave a short half laugh. 'I didn't think anything was more important to you than the island.'

'Which just goes to prove how little you know me!' she retorted on a slightly less collected note.

'So it would seem,' he granted in apparent seriousness. Then, smiling broadly, 'Although you must admit I've been doing my best to rectify my lack of knowledge in that area.'

'Only in order to increase your knowledge of Cowrie, certainly not of me!' she scorned.

He shrugged, and then before she knew it his hand had snaked out to thread within the silken strands of her hair, propelling her closer. 'Okay, I'll show an undivided interest in you, then, if that's what you would prefer,' he proposed lazily.

'No!' Devon immediately protested in a panic even though she was unsure whether he actually meant to do anything of the kind, or whether he was simply being annoying again. Pushing away from him, she heaved a sigh of relief on finding herself at liberty. 'And—and that isn't why I came after you! It was in order to tell you to mind your own business and to stop encouraging Dad in his foolhardy idea of sailing off on his own!'

His deep blue eyes, several shades darker now in the dim light, swept over her sardonically. 'That sounds more like you. Just because the idea doesn't find favour in your eyes, you consider it an unwarranted interference if anyone else disagrees.'

'No, that's not it at all!' she denied half defensively, half indignantly. Once again he was insinuating she was selfish, when actually all her concern was for her father. 'I'm against it because he doesn't happen to be well enough to undertake such a trip, if you must know!'

'Only in your opinion, apparently. Matt appears to consider he's well and able enough.'

'Well, his doctor doesn't!'

'Oh? That's not what I was told. In fact, according to Matt the doctor simply advised a break from his heavy workload here,' he emphasised meaningfully, 'and then to take things a little easier.'

'And you think a solo yachting voyage comes under the classification of taking it easy, do you?' she scoffed caustically.

'If he approaches it in slow stages there's no reason why it shouldn't be. He's obviously competent enough to know what he's doing.'

His last remark was much the same as Garth had made while they were down at the camp, and so was her reply. 'It's also very difficult to be competent if you're not even capable of standing on your feet!' she snapped. 'I mean, you do realise the reason the doctor advocated he try not to do so much was because he thought a heart condition could be developing, don't you?'

Hunt's shapely mouth firmed somewhat. 'I also realise "could be" is a long way from "has"!' he countered succinctly. 'And perhaps if he is relieved of both his financial worries and his workload, you may even find the "could be" in doubt also.'

'Oh, yes, it's in your own interests to say that, isn't it?' Devon accused, disparagement uppermost. 'After all, the thought of his being in a position to afford the type of boat he's always wanted is just another lever for you to use in order to achieve your aims, isn't it?'

'No, it is not!' His sharply voiced denial was catergorical. 'And I wouldn't be making too many of those wild accusations either if I were you, sweetheart, or you may really find yourself with a battle on your hands!'

A battle he would somehow ensure she had no hope of winning, no doubt! she surmised wrathfully. However, the thought did have her moderating her tone a little—although not appreciably the astringent intonation contained therein. 'Then why *are* you supporting the scheme so adamantly?' she challenged.

'Mainly, because it's obviously been a life-long ambition of his, and it's just as evident he feels that, due to his age, if he doesn't make a move shortly, then he very likely never will be able to fulfil his dream . . . which, I might add, clearly means a great deal to him!' he stressed forcefully.

Devon touched even white teeth to her lip diffidently. She also knew how much her father's plan meant to him, but that still didn't necessarily make it advisable, did it? 'Yes—well—it's also been a life-long ambition of mine to have my father live for as many years as possible,' she retorted in defence.

His eyes didn't waver from hers by so much as a fraction. 'Even to the extent of being willing to sink the ship completely in order to put out the fire, it would appear.'

'And just what's that supposed to mean?' she flared, sensing more criticism.

'It means, that because you fear he *might* suddenly die at sea, you would rather kill him for sure by preventing him from going at all!' she was informed in hard-edged accents.

'That's not true!' she cried resentfully. 'And—and you have no basis for claiming his not going would bring about anything of the kind! It hasn't in the past, so why should it in the future?'

'Because the difference is, the minute he leaves this island he's going to have nothing to do . . . except pine for what his over-protective daughter is wanting to deny him!' He paused, his expression unrelenting. 'And don't try telling me he won't, because even if you are too obstinate to admit it, you know damned well he will!'

Just as leaving the island would create a similar void in all their lives! 'But with you accepting none of the blame, of course!' she gibed bitterly.

Hunt shook his head in disbelief. 'Why the hell should I?'

'Because it's all your fault! If you hadn't come here none of these decisions would be necessary!'

'No, he'd be considering sailing off in that old sloop of his instead! At least this way he can afford to have a decent boat under him fitted out with the best equipment available!'

Devon stared at him fiercely, her breasts rising and falling rapidly with the strength of her feelings. 'Oh, God, I detest you!' she choked. And not only because all her troubles had begun with his arrival, but because he also seemed to have an answer for everything! Abruptly, her eyes misted. 'You don't care how many lives you ruin as long as you can *develop*,' with tearful acrimony, 'an area, do you?'

Apart from a muscle that flickered briefly beneath the sun-darkened skin of his jaw, Hunt's demeanour didn't alter. 'I'd hardly call it ruining a person's life to rescue them from obvious financial straits, and at the same time provide them with the means to achieve what they've always longed to do!'

Okay, so maybe there were a number of reasons her father wasn't averse to the deal, but there were others concerned too, weren't there? she reasoned defiantly, blinking away her tears. 'And Aunt Violet? She doesn't want to leave here either—as you probably already know, and was doubtless the reason you were so busily buttering her up this afternoon! She won't know what to do with herself once there's no guests for her to feed up and fuss over.'

He nodded contemplatively. 'Hmm. . . . Except in that regard I could have plans for Aunt Vi,' he caught her offguard by suddenly musing.

'Oh, and what sort of plans would they be?' she demanded on a suspicious note. Now what was going on in that contriving mind of his?

'W-e-ll,' he lengthened the word thoughtfully—or was it deliberately suspensefully? fumed Devon, 'naturally we'd require staff if everything pans out as I envisage, and if that meal she provided tonight is any indication, then with an increased and more modern range of equipment plus a few helpers, I suspect we would really see Aunt Vi's true colours come to the fore and we'd find ourselves with one hell of a fine chef on our hands.' Halting, he tilted his head quizzically. 'Think she'd be interested?'

Oh, yes, she'd certainly be interested all right! Would probably jump at the chance, in fact, Devon admitted with a sigh. And there would go any opposition she may have been able to extract from her aunt concerning the sale! To the man with her, though, she merely offered a deprecating hunching of her shoulders.

'I wouldn't know,' she alleged listlessly. 'You'd have to ask her that yourself.' Then, with her voice strengthening, 'But we appear to have digressed. I came out here to talk about Dad, not to discuss any new plans you may be hatching.'

'You're not interested in learning if I have anything in mind for you too, then?' he drawled.

Devon's fingers clenched. 'I already know all I want to in that regard. You're doing your best to deprive me of my home as soon as possible. Isn't that enough?' And inhaling deeply, 'Now to return to. . .'

'You wouldn't prefer to work here rather than leave altogether?' he broke in on her idly. 'After all, you do have a thorough knowledge of all the attractions here that would be hard, if not almost impossible, for anyone else to duplicate.'

Momentarily, her heart leapt at the thought of remaining, and then it spiralled downwards again. 'That's the carrot that's supposed to hopefully put paid to all my opposition, is it?' she jeered. 'Well, you can forget it! Cowrie means more to me than simply somewhere to work! Besides, since you put it that way, yes, I would rather leave than ever be employed by you, Hunter Kincaid!' Especially if it meant all her special places on the island would be private no longer.

'Oh, don't be so childish!' he slated. 'That's just cutting off your nose to spite your face, and you know it. Nor was it an attempt to stifle your opposition. I figure I can already do that without resorting to such means,' with his lips twitching wryly. 'It was simply an offer I considered would benefit us both.'

Perhaps he was telling the truth, perhaps not. It really didn't matter. 'Well, whatever the reason, my answer still isn't about to change,' she shrugged. 'The island just wouldn't be the same, and I'd rather n-not be here to see it h-happening.' Her voice began to shake ominously and, looking away, she drew a steadying breath before continuing. 'In—in any event, there's still Garth to consider.'

Hunt made a contemptuous sound deep in his throat. 'I don't know why! What consideration has he ever shown you?'

'You wouldn't know!' She swung back to face him

now, balefully. 'And whether you approve of him or not, he still does happen to be my fiancé!'

'You wouldn't know it from looking at the pair of you,' he declared drily. 'Just because you've evidently known each other all your lives doesn't mean you're supposed to act as if you've been married that long as well, you know. Instead of that half-hearted apology for a wave he gave you on leaving, *this* is what he should have been doing!' He suddenly swept her against his hard, muscular outline, his arms imprisoning her as a hand reached up to cradle and immobilise her head, his lips claiming hers with a sensuousness she was helpless to overcome.

In no time at all it seemed her initial flustered struggles had given way to an even more disturbing response. It was as if she had lost all control over her emotions whenever he kissed her, and all they wanted to do was answer in kind the drugging demands of his possessive mouth. Compulsively, her lips parted, inviting his further exploration, a shiver of unexpectedly fervent feeling shooting through her when he did so. Then without warning, and just as abruptly as he had pulled her to him, Hunt now put her away from him.

'That's how engaged couples usually say good-bye,' he drawled in a roughly bantering manner.

Striving desperately to appear as unaffected by the encounter as he apparently was, despite experiencing an overwhelming need to take to her heels, Devon returned his indolently scanning gaze as steadily as possible. 'You speak from the experience of having a fiancée yourself, do you?' something quite unaccountable made her challenge.

'Uh-uh!' he grinned and gave a negative shake of his head. 'Promises to marry have never been in my line.'

Meaning, no doubt, that he'd never found it necessary to offer marriage in order to get what he wanted! she deduced with a grimace. Her chin angled unconsciously higher. 'In that case, as far as engaged couples' behaviour is concerned, it would appear my knowledge is greater than yours, then, wouldn't it?' she asserted, sweetly mocking, and took her leave purposefully, while she was still on top.

'Although obviously not in experience,' she heard him laugh after her.

'Thankfully!' she retorted implicitly over her shoulder, but didn't stop until she reached the verandah. Then, involuntarily almost, she cast a swift look back, and received a taunting salute for her pains, whereupon she promptly spun about and hurried into her bedroom.

It wasn't until some time afterwards when she found herself mulling over their conversation as she prepared for sleep that she suddenly realised in some surprise that, in the main, there had been a complete absence of his normal goading, and she spared a thought to wonder why. Moreover, she couldn't make up her mind whether it had been an improvement or not. When all was said and done, the lack of it definitely hadn't appeared to make her any more successful in winning an argument against him than she usually was when it was present! she noted with a disgruntled expression as she punched her pillow into a more comfortable shape with unnecessary vigour.

In the morning Devon awoke somewhat earlier than usual and deciding it would be pleasant to have an early breakfast alone with her father for a change, showered swiftly and donned a pair of red shorts

together with a white strapless, midriff top, and set off
for the kitchen. On passing the dining room, however,
she came to a stunned halt on seeing Hunt calmly
ensconsed at the table with her parent and partaking of
a hearty meal.

Since her appearance had obviously caught their
attention she then had no choice but to enter the room
and respond to their greetings, although now she
would have preferred to keep going and eat alone in
the kitchen.

'Come to join us, love, have you?' Granville smiled
fondly. 'That's nice. Pull up a chair.'

With nothing for it but to do as he suggested,
Devon took a seat opposite them, reluctantly, her gaze
expressive as it came to rest on the younger man.
'Have you moved in here?' she enquired with a forced
smile for her father's benefit, but with just enough
causticity for the recipient of her query to get the
message.

Hunt's mouth took on a wry curve. 'It's a tempting
thought, but as it happens I arrived early, so my
adopted aunt invited me to have some breakfast.'

'They don't feed you on the *Kanandah*?' Her eyes
widened, eloquently gibing.

'Mmm,' he owned laconically. 'But it's hard to
refuse one of Aunt Vi's meals.'

Besides which his sizeable frame would undoubtedly require some filling, she speculated sardonically, and not a little put out by his continued
reference to her aunt as Vi. Why should he be
permitted such familiarity, particularly when Garth
hadn't even been invited to progress beyond a
formal Miss Matthews after all the years he'd known
her? Moodily, she poured herself a cup of tea from

the pot already on the table and began buttering a piece of golden toast.

'So what made you arrive this early, then?' she asked of Hunt at length.

Beneath their dark green, tank top covering, his shoulders flexed powerfully. 'Seeing we've got a lot of ground to cover today, I thought an early as possible start would be expedient.'

'In fact, Violet's packing a lunch for you both right now so there won't be any need for you to interrupt your tour,' put in her father informatively.

Devon would have preferred the welcome respite a return to the house for the meal would have provided! 'That is thoughtful of her,' she smiled hollowly. 'Although she really needn't have bothered. I mean, I have to return to help her with the guests' lunches, in any case.'

'Oh, no, not now there's only four of them. Violet says she'll be able to manage on her own without any trouble at all,' he unwittingly destroyed her hopes. 'No, you and Hunt make a full day of it, then you're not likely to miss anything.'

Uncertain whether anything had been intended by that last comment, Devon slanted him a searching, sideways glance. 'As if I would,' she murmured, though somewhat tongue-in-cheek.

'Oh, I wasn't suggesting that at all,' he hastened to assure her earnestly, although she couldn't quite keep a light flush from staining her cheeks when she intercepted a graphic, brow-raised gaze from the man beside him. 'It's just that you've seen it all so many times before that what you might now consider unexceptional could prove to be very interesting to someone who hasn't seen it previously.'

'Mmm, maybe,' she was prepared to concede, meditatively. Her glance shifted so that it centred fully on Hunt. 'I can see I shall just have to point out to you every solitary thing I can think of, won't I?' And thereby fill his head with so much trivia that he would hopefully tire of his tour very swiftly! 'So where would you like to begin? With a climb to the top of The Pinnacle?'

'Uh-uh!' His ensuing veto may have been brief, but at the same time it was unmistakably decisive. 'I think the reef first, while there's still sufficient water covering it to enable us to do some snorkelling, otherwise the tide will be low again if we leave it until after we've seen The Pinnacle.'

Foiled again, grimaced Devon in disgust, but refusing to allow her disappointment to show. 'The reef it is, then.' She gave a creditably indifferent shrug. 'Although I do hope you have your own gear because we don't have any spares except Dad's, and I doubt his flippers, especially, would fit you.'

'No worries,' he averred on a dry note. 'As a matter of fact I did bring mine with me. They're outside the back door.'

'That's fortunate,' she lauded with extremely suspect pleasure before concentrating her increasingly vexed thoughts on her meal once more. Already she could tell it was going to be one of *those* days!

Immediately breakfast was concluded, Devon returned to her room in order to slip on an ice blue and cerise bikini before replacing her shorts and top, and to gather up her snorkelling gear. Hunt was talking to her aunt in the kitchen when she arrived at that room, and from the unquestionably delighted look on that woman's face it wasn't difficult to guess just what had been the topic of their discussion.

'I gather you've spoken to Aunt Violet about her staying on,' she consequently said to Hunt as they left the house and she retrieved a couple of towels from the laundry as they passed.

He nodded. 'Apparently the idea appeals to her greatly.'

Exactly as she had thought it would! 'Another one to you, huh?' she quipped with as much feigned unconcern as she could evince.

'You would rather she was miserable too at having to leave just because that's what you're determined to do?' He was back to being his mocking, as well as reproving this time, self again.

'Of course not!' she denied, but a little uncomfortably. She supposed that was how it could have sounded, although naturally she was glad for her aunt's sake. She simply hated to see him have yet another victory, that was all! With a dispirited sigh, she led the rest of the way down to the beach in silence.

Once there, Devon peeled off her outer garments and, catching up her apparatus, walked quickly down to the water. If she was going to have to go through with this, she may as well get it over and done with as rapidly as she could. A few moments later Hunt joined her, his hip-hugging swimming shorts revealing an even longer length of strongly muscled, brown leg than his covering shorts had done, and suddenly aware her covert gaze was turning into an interestedly assessing one, she hurriedly cleaned and rinsed her mask before pulling both it and her snorkel into place, and then moved out into slightly deeper water to dispose of any sand in her flippers before sliding them on to her feet.

'Ready?' she asked flatly as soon as he had followed suit, and immediately he nodded pushed herself off from the bottom and began heading out through the lagoon without waiting to see if he was as accustomed to this type of swimming as she was.

It soon became apparent he was by the ease with which he caught up with her, and as they slowly propelled themselves through the glistening water side by side she discovered, as she had many times before, that the tranquillity of the scene below seemed to have the power to clear and soothe the mind until all that remained was a limitless wonder and enjoyment of her surroundings.

As they swam, myriad varieties of fish glided past tamely; shoals of silvery black-spot sea perch, peacock wrasses, brown, blue and black-banded tuskfish, large red coral cods with their distinctive blue dots, yellow and black butterfly fish, together with a host of others. But it was to the numerous blue and green parrot fishes, gnawing at the massive boulders of coral that were interspersed across the lagoon's sandy floor, that Devon impulsively pointed and, by signalling, indicated that Hunt should stop and listen. In the absolute quiet that followed the noise of the fishes' beak-like jaws scraping at and breaking off pieces of coral to obtain the polyps and worms that lived within was easy to hear, and Hunt gave an almost disbelieving shake of his head before they continued on.

As soon as they were above the mass of the surrounding reef itself, Devon began a series of duck-dives in order to point out other things of interest; velvety mantled reef clams, each one a richly different colour; orange and white anemone fish sheltering within gently swaying, brightly tinted tentacles; fat, sluggish-looking *bêche-de-mer*; exquisite wine-red, orange and green feather stars; royal blue starfish and needle-spined sea urchins; large brown cushion sponges, bright yellow inside, and a red hermit crab in a large triton shell; brilliant blue and black tangs, blue-green damsel fish, Moorish idols, and gloriously marked angelfish; and of course the breath-taking beauty of the multi-hued coral itself in both its hard and soft forms.

Everywhere they went there was something different to be seen, perhaps the best part being that, due to no fishing ever being permitted on the inner reefs, none of the so very varied life forms hurried away at their approach but allowed them to swim among them, even to hold some of the fishes in their hands, and because Hunt's interest was so oviously genuine, to the extent of indicating things to her that he thought she may have missed—and so completely opposite in attitude to Garth when she had attempted to share such an underwater paradise with him—Devon found herself revealing much, much more than she had originally intended and, to her amazement, deriving considerable pleasure from doing so.

However, as they neared the reef front where the coral plunged steeply thirty fathoms or more to the seabed below, she still couldn't quite bring herself to warn him of the, to some people, startling sight that was about to confront him. It was one of those few chances she had to catch him unawares for once and she was curious, if nothing else, to see how he would react to it. As she recalled, ruefully, one look had been sufficient for Garth and he hadn't been able to return to the security of the lagoon quickly enough, and subconsciously, she was half hopeful that would be the response of her companion today as well.

As it turned out, Hunt demonstrated no such desire on seeing the reef abruptly drop away beneath him, leaving him in the deeper blue waters of the open ocean, although after continuing seaward for a few yards he did surface. With a partly disappointed, partly ill-concealed impish look on her face, Devon did the same.

Pushing his mask to the top of his head and removing his snorkel, he fixed her with an askance gaze. 'You'll keep, young lady, you'll keep!' he vowed in a, not altogether pseudo, menacing drawl.

'Why? What did I do?' she queried innocently, but unable to entirely restrain the humorous curve playing about her lips. 'You said you wanted to see everything, and some of the best corals are always found on the outer edge of a reef.'

'I think perhaps you'd better show me then,' he advocated drily, almost as if he didn't believe her.

'I was going to,' she claimed as she re-adjusted her mask. Followed by an irrepressible, 'Provided you stayed around long enough to have a look, that was,' just before inserting her snorkel and swiftly diving.

Hunt followed her just as quickly and found she hadn't been exaggerating. Some of the most attractive coral growths were located along the sides of that nearly straight-sided drop. Among them the fiery red, lacy fan coral, while here too even greater varieties of multi-tinted fish darted and whirled amidst the coloured stems, and in and out of hidden crevices.

This was also the habitat of most of the larger species of reef fish and on this occasion it was Devon who received a shock on suddenly turning and discovering the enormous head of a giant Queensland groper—its great maw of a mouth opening and closing slowly—not more than a yard or so away from her. It wasn't the first time she had come across him—in fact, a pair of them had made the island's reef their home— but it was the first time she had come face to face with him so abruptly. Normally the species wasn't aggressive towards humans, its diet consisting mainly of crustaceans and other fish, but they were exceptionally inquisitive, and to have its eight-foot long form nosing around for the whole time you remained in their particular territory was somewhat unnerving, and so, with an expressive signal to Hunt advising him of their unwanted company, she reluctantly headed for the surface once more and set off for the shallower water above the reef.

By now the tide had receded noticeably, and as they made their way back leisurely towards the reef flats Devon began directing Hunt's attention towards the many and varied shells that seemed to carpet every sandy space; red-lipped and purple-mounted strombs; pale orange and coffee coloured spider shells; volutes of every description; delicately patterned, but poison- ous, cone shells; ram's horns that had been washed up from deeper waters during storms; Bailer, trochus, and cockle shells; and of course numerous examples of those that had given the island its name, including egg, tiger, and small ring cowries in all their different variations of colour.

'Well, what did you think of it?' she asked when they at last returned to the shallows and removed their gear, and for the first time speaking to him in a totally natural vein.

'Incredible!' Hunt's reply was short but sincere.

'And so are you as a guide. You really know your subject and what you're doing out there, don't you, sweetheart?'

The unexpected compliment had her executing a deprecating half shrug as she began leaving the water. 'As a Chairman of the Board, you don't make a bad skindiver yourself,' she quipped wryly. And with her gaze resting on him quizzically as they ambled across the sand, 'You've done quite a bit of diving before, haven't you?'

He nodded. 'Like you, I was also born and raised close to the sea and I've been mucking about in boats and diving for almost as long as I can remember.'

So that explained his expertise! Finger-combing her hair into place, she didn't quite look at him as she probed diffidently, 'Whereabouts by the sea?'

'Mooloolaba, on the Sunshine Coast just north of Brisbane,' he relayed casually, shaking the water from his own hair and then raking a hand through it before dropping down on to one of the towels she had brought along.

Devon spread the other towel out a short distance away and sank down on to it in a thoughtful pose with her arms linking loosely about her updrawn legs, her chin resting on her knees. 'You must miss it, then, now that your business is conducted from Brisbane,' she ventured. Her father having informed her that that was where the Eastern Development Corporation was based.

'Uh-uh!' He moved his head lazily. 'Our main office is in Brisbane and I commute by helicopter when I have to, but our head office is still on the Sunshine Coast. It's one of the fastest growing areas in the State and we still get a lot of work from that district . . .

apart from the fact that I prefer to continue living there.'

She gazed out to sea for a moment, her thoughts confused. She didn't know why she should be interested in his background, but strangely she was. 'And—and your firm is a family concern, is it?' She couldn't think of any other circumstances that would permit him to reach the position he had at such an early age.

'No, all my own work,' he advised matter-of-factly, but with a humorous tilt to his mouth as if he sensed the reasoning behind her question. 'When I was a kid it always used to alternate between feast and famine in our house—with famine predominating.' The upward curve of his lips became more ruefully pronounced. 'My old man's passion for punting on the horses saw to that.'

Devon's eyes shaded with sympathy. Just by what he left out she suspected his early years had been far rougher than she could ever imagine. 'Th-then how . . .?'

'Did I make it to Chairman of the Board?' He hunched his wide shoulders in a deprecating gesture. 'With a little hard work, and a lot of good luck, I guess.'

After what he'd just had to say, she was inclined to think it was more likely to have been vice versa. 'For example?'

'For example . . .' Hunt suddenly reached across to wrap a hand around the far side of her neck and by exerting pressure on it pulled her off-balance so that she half fell towards him, 'I'm still deciding just what punishment you deserve to have meted out to you for that little trick of yours out there,' he smiled mock-threateningly into her wide-eyed and somewhat startled features.

'Why, did it frighten you?' she dared to taunt as she laughingly struggled to regain her previous position, in vain.

'No, it didn't frighten me,' he declared wryly as he pushed her down on to the sand and kept her pinned there by a hand on each shoulder. 'Nonetheless, as you damn well know, it is a trifle unsettling to be looking at vividly coloured fish and an assortment of coral one moment ... and then staring into a seemingly bottomless blue pit the next!'

Her turquoise eyes sparkled impenitently. For some unknown reason she appeared to have lost her nervousness of him this morning. Perhaps because the mood of affinity that had developed between them while viewing the reef hadn't yet dissipated.

'I—well—since you were obviously an experienced skindiver, I thought you would no doubt know what to expect,' she alleged mirthfully.

'Just like you were anticipating the appearance of that groper that had you nearly jumping out of your skin, hmm?' he teased in turn.

She could hardly deny it. 'He is huge, isn't he?' she grinned expressively instead.

He raised his brows slightly at her wording. 'You've seen him before, then?'

'And his mate,' she nodded. 'They've got a cave down there somewhere where they've set up home. In fact, they've been here quite a few years now. Just about all the reefs have their pair of guardian gropers.'

'Mmm, so I've heard.'

Her lips formed a disappointed pout. 'So you were expecting to see something of the kind?'

'Not entirely,' he owned, eloquently dry. 'Originally, I was under the impression we would only be exploring the top of the reef. However, immediately we moved into deeper water I knew there was a distinct possibility some of the larger species could suddenly put in an appearance.'

'The first time I saw him I nearly swallowed my snorkel in shock,' she now confessed with a grin. 'I'd been told what large heads and mouths they possess, but until you actually see one for yourself nothing can prepare you for just *how* huge those gaping mouths are!'

The whole time she had been talking Hunt's gaze had been fastened to her softly contoured lips, and now he brushed his thumb across her lower one slowly. 'While yours is quite beautiful, particularly when you smile like that,' he murmured with a more resonant nuance than she had ever detected in his voice before.

All at once Devon tensed warily, her expression faltering beneath the intensity of his. In almost as many minutes he had twice changed the direction of their conversation, but this time his demeanour had altered perceptibly too, and thereby resurrected all her previous feelings of disturbing vulnerability.

'Hunt—I . . . no!' Only the last was unhesitatingly voiced as his head lowered to hers and she began to struggle in earnest now. 'Stop it! You have no. . .'

His lips closing inexorably over hers effectively brought an end to her partly commanding, partly panicking protest, and as he slid a pillowing—or restraining?—arm beneath her head and drew her slender form closer to the rugged masculinity of his, her heart began pounding raggedly. She was only too aware of the response he was capable of engendering within her, but even more disconcerting was the knowledge that he was unquestionably aware of it also! He appeared to totally disregard the fact that she was engaged, and he therefore had no right to keep kissing her as he did, but, oh God, did he also have to be so skilfully practised that he made her ignore it as well? she despaired on feeling her senses start to swim as his warm and knowing mouth trailed a scorching path to the throbbing hollow at the base of her throat, and knew herself to be surrendering helplessly once more.

Hunt smoothed an arousing hand leisurely over her hip and upwards, seeking the deep indentation of her waist before, with fingers spreading, moving it unhurriedly across her ribs until, finally, bringing it to rest cupping a tautly swelling breast. Feelings she had never before experienced pulsed through Devon, shocking her with their depth so that she trembled and gave a gasp that was somewhere between a moan and a sob. Nothing she had shared with her fiancé had prepared her for this fiery, uncontrollable leaping of the emotions in response to an exploring touch, and she clutched desperately at the sinewed shoulders leaning over her as if seeking something stable in a suddenly rocking world.

Lifting his head, Hunt surveyed her flushed and bewildered features with rueful eyes, his sensuous mouth sloping crookedly. 'You really are an innocent aren't you, sweetheart?' he mused wryly.

A deeper, brighter stain of embarrassment joined the colour already tinting Devon's cheeks and she averted her face swiftly. 'So you keep inferring!' she heaved. He made her feel like some gauche and maladjusted adolescent! Forcing herself to look back at him, her eyes smouldered resentfully. 'Because it's a supposition that enables you to amuse yourself at Garth's and my expense, no doubt!'

'I don't know about amused, but I sure am amazed,' he amended drily. 'What kind of a man is he, this fiancé of yours, that he can be engaged to someone with your looks and so very shapely figure and yet apparently make no attempt to make love to you?'

'One who *is* capable of exercising some self-control, obviously!' she sniped explicitly.

'Much to your disappointment, presumably, if your response a while ago was any indication,' he immediately mocked on a drawling note and had her face reddening anew. She should have known better than to attempt to put him in his place when her own inexcusable behaviour had left her open to just such mortifying remarks. 'Perhaps I could do you a favour by telling him what he's missing.'

'Don't you dare!' she burst out, aghast. She could believe him capable of doing it, if only to discomfort Garth.

'He wouldn't understand?' came the innocent-sounding, but subtly toned question.

How could she expect him to? She didn't even understand herself why she appeared to have no defences whatsoever against this man. 'Would you, if the positions were reversed?' she countered with some asperity.

He smiled indolently. 'Sweetheart, if I was engaged to you I'd be making damned sure there'd be no reason for you to be looking to another man to cater to any of your needs because I'd be well and truly seeing to them myself, believe me!'

He probably could too, she conceded, grudgingly, even though she hadn't meant if the position had been reversed specifically with regard to Garth. Nonetheless ... 'And—and neither am I looking for someone to cater to any of my needs now, as you put it!' she protested heatedly. 'You're the one who keeps grabbing hold of me, not the other way around!'

'You, merely employing the most novel method of rejection I've ever encountered, hmm?'

Devon turned her face away again, chewing at her lip discomfitedly. Did he always have to be quite so ruthlessly forthright? 'I—well—since you keep imply-ing I suffer from a lack of it, maybe I just figured I should make the most of the opportunities you so obligingly present me with to gain more experience,' she parried with a protective flippancy.

Hunt's sable-framed eyes glinted with lazy provoca-tion. 'In which event, it's doubtless just as well I don't practise such a rigid self-control as your inestimable fiancé.'

'No, it is not!' she refuted in no little dismay. Oh, lord, what had she done now? Unwittingly insinuated the very opposite to what she really wanted? 'I'm more than content with matters as they are—or as they *were* until you arrived,' she inserted hastily in order to make her position quite clear, 'so—so now, if you feel you've amused yourself sufficiently for one morning, I'd be glad if you would let go of me.' Her voice became tinged with defensive sarcasm as she began straining away from him. 'Thanks to you I'm now covered in sand, and I'd like to wash it off.'

With an unruffled grin, he resumed his sitting position, but continued to eye her humorously as she scrambled hurriedly to her feet. 'I could always brush it off, if you would prefer,' he drawled.

Devon simply replied with a nettled glare and set off for the deepest water available in the lagoon now that the tide was just about at its lowest. It wasn't only the sand she felt in need of washing away now, but also the disturbing image of his hands moving freely over her smooth skin which his last bantering offer had waywardly implanted in her mind.

Later, after having returned their snorkelling gear to the house and collected the picnic lunch Violet had prepared, they began the climb towards the top of The Pinnacle. Only now Devon's former feeling of companionship towards the man accompanying her had dissipated entirely, and although she didn't attempt to deliberately hide anything from him, the spontaneity and enthusiasm that had been present during their exploration of the reef weren't in evidence, her information brief and supplied in an offhand manner.

As ever, the panorama visible from the peak was magnificent, providing as it did an uninterrupted view of the whole island together with its surrounding coral, as well as the long, foam-swept ribbon reefs in the far distance that denoted the outer barrier as the incoming swells from the misnamed Pacific broke over them rhythmically. Behind their protective edges, to landward, the azure water was calmer, with only an occasional surge of white to indicate the presence of other formations that could prove so treacherous to the unknowledgeable, while to the south a few smaller, uninhabited islands could be seen on the horizon, the whole outlook glittering brilliantly beneath a cloudless blue sky.

They had lunch in the shade of a young coconut

palm a little way down from the peak, and as he bit
absently into a crisp apple afterwards, Hunt looked
over the seascape again contemplatively before settling
his gaze on Devon's slightly moody countenance.

'So you don't really get much of a view from up
here, huh?' he reminded her on a sardonic note of her
original contention when she had taken him out to
Rocky Point.

'Just a case of familiarity having bred contempt, I
suppose,' she excused with a shrug.

'And the graves, and the cave paintings? Was it
familiarity that made you forget to mention them too?'

'I guess it must have been,' she wasn't above
claiming. 'Although you've seen them all now, so I
really can't see what difference it makes.'

'Except that from here I can also see another two or
three coves north of Careen Beach that, to date, I also
haven't heard mentioned or seen.'

Devon glanced towards the area herself, as much to
avoid his penetrating gaze as anything. 'You hadn't
heard of the mangroves either until we went there but
you didn't particularly want to see them,' she
temporised evasively.

'Meaning, those coves don't have much to recommend them?'

Aware his eyes were still focused intently in her
direction, she shifted restively and studiously made
certain their glances didn't connect. 'Well, no, not
exactly,' she admitted awkwardly. Then, on a more
defiant note, 'I just thought you'd be able to discover
at least some of the island without my help!'

'Despite knowing Matt was expecting you to show
me *everything* Cowrie has to offer?' Hunt's expression
assumed a satirically disbelieving cast.

Devon heaved a disgruntled breath. 'I didn't realise that would mean my spending almost every waking minute in your company, though!' she grimaced.

Her mutinous outburst brought a disarming smile to his lips, and had her wishing inconsequentially that he wasn't so damned good looking. However, instead of making some goading retort, as she was half expecting, he merely concentrated his attention on what apparently interested him most by assuming, 'Both coves being much the same as Careen Beach, then?'

Relief, that he hadn't commented on her last rankled remark—with disastrous results from her standpoint, no doubt—plus a certain lingering disconcertion, had her answering unthinkingly and, in consequence, more informatively than she had done for some time.

'Sandy Bay, the first one is, but Shell Beach—it's only one really, not two—is a little different. It has only a narrow passage between the reef and the beach, which means of course that it's not so good for just swimming, but not surprisingly in view of its name, that's really the one to go to if you want to see the largest variety of shells, and especially after a storm when different ones are washed up from the deep,' she relayed.

'I see.' Hunt's mouth took on an oblique slant. 'It would appear your services as a guide don't finish today, after all, then.' And when she didn't reply—wouldn't was more like it, 'Matt was also telling me this happens to be a favoured turtle breeding ground. Something else that just slipped your mind?' A sceptically quirking brow spoke volumes.

Now Devon did deign to answer, challengingly. 'Yes, as a matter of fact, it did!' she flared, and quite truthfully. 'Even though the season's almost finished, some late ones have still been arriving on the night tide during the last couple of weeks in order to lay their eggs, but due to having a considerable amount on my mind this last few days,' tartly expressed, 'I haven't checked for signs of any more of them having come ashore and, as a result, clean forgot about them!'

'Okay, one to you this time,' he laughed, holding up a hand in a gesture of submission. 'That should make us square for the day . . . and be reason enough for a return of that smile of yours, shouldn't it?'

Struck once again by his ready good humour—she suspected Garth wouldn't be prepared to forgive and forget anywhere near so easily—it was impossible for Devon's normally sunny nature not to assert itself in response and the corners of her soft mouth suddenly started to curve upwards.

'That's more like it,' Hunt promptly approved, and creating within her an oddly pleased feeling she could only be rid of by giving herself a severe mental shake. With his folded arms resting across updrawn knees, he went on idly, 'Matt also informs me you have quite an extensive array of shells at the house. I'd be interested to see them if I could.'

The beginnings of Devon's smile faded abruptly. 'They're not for sale, if that's what you've got in mind,' she informed him tightly.

'So who suggested they were?' He rubbed a hand part way round his neck and shook his head in patent incredulity. 'Hell! What have I done to make you so suspicious of everything I damn well say?'

Thinking about it, she couldn't have said for certain. In fact, if she was really honest, she'd concede that any underhand tactics so far had all been perpetrated by herself, not him. A subconscious ploy just to hopefully keep him at that safe distance? she now wondered. Not that it seemed to have been particularly successful, the rueful thought immediately followed, and had her dipping her head uncomfortably.

'All right, I—I'm sorry,' she apologised in jerky accents. But feeling obliged to at least try to be as pleasant in defeat as he had been, half smiled whimsically, 'I guess that makes it two to one in your favour now.'

His answering smile had her senses reeling. 'I'd rather just see your collection of shells,' he averred gently.

'That too, then,' she suddenly found herself allowing.

'Now?'

'If—if you like, and if there's—there's nothing else you want to see round here.' She waved a hand about her somewhat distractedly as she fought to recover her equilibrium.

'It should finish the day off very nicely,' he contended, swiftly consigning the remains from their lunch to the basket before rising lithely to his feet and extending a helping hand towards her.

Accepting it, Devon released it again as soon as she was upright. 'I noticed before that the *Kanandah*'s not at her mooring. Where's she gone?' she enquired in an effort to camouflage her still inexplicably unsettled emotions.

'To Northport, for extra supplies. We're giving a barbecue tomorrow night and everyone on the island's invited,' he informed her, casually.

'To celebrate . . .'

'As return hospitality for all that's been extended to us since our arrival,' was the purposeful interposition Then, as an addition, as if guessing what her reaction would be, 'And I don't want to hear any excuses from you about not attending.'

'Well, I—umm. . .'

'Or I'll be up to the house and carry you down there myself, kicking and screaming all the way, if necessary,' he broke in again to threaten drily.

He would too! Devon knew only too well, and sighed. At the moment both her thoughts and her emotions were far too confused, and confusing, for her to want to spend more time in his company than she absolutely had to, but simultaneously, he obviously didn't intend to take no for an answer.

'Not that I would be kicking and screaming, anyway, but . . . you don't exactly give a person much choice, do you?' she gibed quietly.

Hunt's teasing grin made an indolent appearance. 'How could I when, whether reluctantly given or not, your assistance has probably aided us most?'

'I see,' she acknowledged with a faint nod. Strangely, she found it a somewhat depressing reason.

# CHAPTER SIX

ALTHOUGH she had spent a quite uneventful, but once again unexpectedly enjoyable, morning with Hunt exploring Sandy Bay and Shell Beach by walking over the exposed reef at low tide rather than swimming over it on this occasion, Devon was still not looking forward to attending the barbecue at the bottom camp the following evening—as indicated by the slowness with which she dressed for the affair. Her aunt had long since left together with their guests—though she strongly suspected that woman's early departure was most likely to have been prompted by a desire to lend a helping hand if it was needed—so that only her father and herself still remained at the house.

A knock on her door a few minutes later, however, showed that even he was ready to leave now and with a resigned sigh she pulled her comb through her lightly waving blonde hair one last time before joining him.

'You look appropriately nautical tonight,' Granville smiled as they made their way down the back steps.

Involuntarily, Devon glanced down at her navy blue trim-fitting shorts and matching blue and white striped top. 'Mmm, I suppose I do. I hadn't realised,' she returned ruefully.

'It was very nice of Hunt to think of putting on something like this, though, wasn't it?'

'Mmm.' Her answer was as laconically, as grudgingly, made as her last. She kicked absently at a stone on the path with a sneakered foot, her expression thoughtful. 'He's lucky to be in a position where he can do such things at his age.'

'Fortunate, maybe, but I don't think there was much luck, as such, attached to it. More like a lot of damned hard work as far as I can make out,' he amended on a wry note.

Much as she herself had surmised the day before? 'Oh?' She raised her brows quizzically, promptingly.

He expelled a meditative breath. 'Well, from what Royce was telling me I gather Hunt had something of a hard beginning and that he's been working ever since he was eight or nine. First, after school hours, and then later working for a builder during the day, while also starting up his own industrial cleaning business at night. The latter becoming extremely lucrative in a very short time because he was willing to take on anything and everything, including the dirtiest and at times distinctly dangerous work that no one else was interested in doing. From there he could then begin to utilise that inborn sense he obviously possesses for being able to recognise potential when he sees it, and moved into the development field with a couple of purchases of land that at the time were considered to be almost worthless backblocks, but which now happen to form the centre of a new, thriving community.' He paused, a broad smile shaping his lips. 'And of course, once having made your first million, it becomes progressively easier to make the others that follow.'

Devon nodded silently. Except for the details, it was more or less as she had suspected. Nevertheless, even though she could admire him for his achievements, that didn't make the knowledge that his discerning eyes had now alighted on her island any more acceptable!

'You know, I suppose, that he's already asked Violet to stay on here if he does buy the place?' he now turned to enquire in an evidently pleased tone.

She nodded again. 'While you're envisioning sailing off on your own in a lovely brand new boat, no doubt!' She couldn't stop all signs of her antipathy towards the idea from showing.

He didn't deny it, but merely suggested quietly, 'You could always come with me.'

The temptation to do so was strong, if only in order to keep an eye on his health, except for one thing. 'And Garth? What's he supposed to do in the meantime, wait patiently for his fiancée to condescend to return?' She slanted him a sardonic look. 'Or are you now going to suggest that he comes too?'

'Hardly!' he half laughed, half snorted. 'You know as well as I do that Garth doesn't know the difference between a jib and a gybe, and we'd be lucky to even clear the channel with him giving a hand. That is, if we could manage to part him from his books long enough to join in to that extent.'

Unfortunately, he wasn't wrong, and she couldn't restrain a wry smile in acknowledgment. 'Besides, I thought your whole idea was to do it single-handed,' she put forward with a sigh.

'Well, yes, it is really,' he conceded. But with a quickly added, 'Although I'd have no objections to you coming along if you really wanted to.' His eyes twinkled abruptly. 'I never have particularly liked preparing food, as you know.'

'Oh, thanks!' she retorted drily. 'In other words, you'd only want me along as head cook and bottle washer, is that it?'

'No, I was only joking,' he chuckled. 'You should

know you're the only one I would want with me, in any capacity. Although as Hunt was only saying this morning, with a new boat. . .'

Devon didn't hear the remainder of his words. She was too occupied in seething over the fact that Hunt was still apparently encouraging her father in his scheme. How dare he continue to override her wishes just because he didn't happen to see the matter in the same light she did! It was purely a family concern and should have had absolutely nothing to do with him! It was *her* father at risk, not his, so it was easy for him to blithely dismiss the inherent dangers involved and urge her father into fulfilling his ambition. If anything untoward did occur, it certainly wasn't likely to cause *him* any heartbreak! With her head angling higher by the second, she now approached the brightly lantern-lit camp in a less reluctant, but decidedly more belligerent, frame of mind.

The first things they noticed as they entered the clearing were three long tables surrounded by chairs—something else the *Kanandah* had collected from town, Devon deduced—already laden with bowls and platters of salads, cold meats, and seafoods of every description, and the two permanently fixed gas barbecues being industriously supervised by two men she didn't know, but whom she presumed were part of the *Kanandah*'s crew, their cooking plates literally smothered with sizzling, succulent steaks, chops and sausages, which filled the warm night air with an appetising aroma.

Somewhere a stereo was providing background music, anything from disco to classical, a few of the mingling crowd already moving energetically to a currently popular tune, some merely standing or sitting around talking in twos and threes, others handing out an assortment of drinks from huge ice-filled containers.

Observing Royce seated with Stan Noonan, a long-time friend and frequent visitor to the island, Granville was soon heading in their direction once Devon had indicated she would join her aunt, whose help evidently hadn't been needed after all, and a couple of their guests. From where they were seated beneath a long-leaved pandanus she would be close enough to see what was going on, yet just far enough away to remain a little apart from it.

So far, she realised, she hadn't been able to distinguish Hunt's commanding figure among the crowd and she wondered if, for some reason, he was still aboard his yacht. Then no sooner had she finished mulling over his whereabouts than he came into view beside one of the barbecues, his arm draped loosely about attractively sarong-clad Pauline Telfer's bare shoulders, his shapely mouth curving appreciatively in response to what she was laughingly saying.

Oh, yes, now she'd shown him everything he wanted to see on the island, doubtless all his attention would be reserved for the dark-headed girl from now on! Devon denounced acidly, and then gave a horrified gasp, a wave of dismayed colour washing all the way up to her hairline. Dear God, why should she care who he bestowed all his attention on? She was engaged, wasn't she? And not only that, she didn't *want* to have anything more to do with him! By rights, she should have been relieved to see him with the other girl, certainly not nettled or—or resentful! she hesitantly supplied the most accurate word, and promptly wished more than ever that she hadn't come.

As a result of her perturbing reaction, Devon thereafter did her utmost to keep Hunt in sight—solely in order to ensure that wherever he was, she wasn't, and thereby prove to herself, at least, that she was satisfied to be without his company—but only when she had successfully managed to install herself the furthest distance possible away from him at the table for their meal did she feel able to relax a little and thus deliberately ignore his presence altogether as she concentrated, if somewhat uninterestedly, on the food in front of her.

Afterwards, though, it became rather more difficult to retain a watch on his movements, as more of those present began to engage in the, of necessity, casual dancing, and especially as she herself wasn't exactly an unpopular partner. At the conclusion of one such humour-filled circuit of the clearing, Devon stopped to get herself a drink before returning to her seat and suddenly discovered Pauline beside her intent on doing the same, but without Hunt in tow, she noted thankfully.

'So what do you think of the new man in my life? Spunky, eh?' the brunette smiled almost gloatingly as she poured herself a glass of champagne from an already opened bottle standing in an ice bucket.

Devon swallowed convulsively. 'You mean, Hunt, do you?' she queried tautly.

'Well, naturally! Who else?' Pauline smirked in amusement. 'We've been practically inseparable ever since he arrived. And that yacht of his! Have you seen it yet? I have . . . on a number of occasions, actually,' with an archly meaningful look, 'and I can tell you it's out of this world!'

'Yes, I should imagine it would be.' Devon strove to

act unconcernedly. Why should it matter to her how often the other girl had been on the *Kanandah*, or for what purpose? 'It's certainly a beautiful looking boat.'

'As is the owner!' Pauline rolled her eyes expressively. 'I'll bet you've regretted being tied to your fiancé this last couple of days while you've been showing him over the island.'

So she knew about that, did she? But then, it was more than likely everyone did, Devon supposed. 'Not in the slightest, as a matter of fact,' she now answered with a smile of her own, forced though it may have been. 'Personally, I've never cared much for the kind who make it so obvious they're averse to committing themselves.'

'Meaning?' suspiciously.

'Only that I prefer the more reliable type.'

'I meant with regard to Hunt, not what you prefer!' came the impatient clarification.

As Devon had deduced. She gave a vague shrug. 'Well, he is in his early thirties and still very much unattached, after all, and I'd be very surprised if there hadn't been a considerable number of women in his life on the way there. As you said, he *is* good looking, and when coupled with his obvious wealth, I'm sure it's a combination he's become extremely adept at using to his own advantage over the years.'

'Yes, well, I don't know how you, of all people, could make a judgment like that,' Pauline asserted with a dismissive toss of her head. 'I mean, as I was explaining to Hunt only yesterday, stuck way out here all the time as you are, you wouldn't know anything about men with only your father and Garth to gauge by.'

Devon inhaled furiously. They had been discussing

*her*! 'Oh, and just why would you be explaining anything about me to him?'

'Because he asked me about you, that's why,' the other girl laughed insouciantly. 'I don't think he knows what to make of you. You being so prim in your outlook at times where men are concerned, and all. At least, either that, or he just feels sorry for you, I guess.'

Sorry for her! Well, not for trying to deprive her of her home, that was for certain! So what did that leave? That he pitied her for her lack of experience and had therefore set out to do her a favour by broadening her horizons in that regard, and probably providing himself and Pauline with some amusement by discussing them with her afterwards too! She squared her shoulders determinedly.

'Well, you can tell him from me there's no need for him to concern himself on either count,' she declared, refusing to show that in reality she was crying inside with both shame and disappointment. 'As it so happens I couldn't care less whether he can make me out or not, while as for feeling sorry for me . . . well, I suggest he reserves that emotion for himself! With his attitude, I'd say he needs it far more than I ever have!'

'Okay, if that's what you want,' Pauline agreed obligingly.

'I do!' Devon confirmed with a positive nod and, replacing her can of fruit-flavoured mineral water— her throat felt too tight to get anything down it now— she turned on her heel and left the clearing altogether instead of returning to her seat.

Momentarily, she wasn't even aware of which particular direction she was headed, but then the feel of sand underfoot brought her back to her surroundings and, tossing her sneakers on to the ipomea-covered dunes, she continued walking away from the camp along the beach.

'And just where do you think you're going?' Hunt's unmistakable voice suddenly sounded some distance behind her.

'To look for turtles,' she said the first thing that came to mind, without stopping.

'It's a bit early for that, isn't it? The tide won't be full for almost another two hours yet.'

She wasn't sure but she thought his voice sounded closer that time and she increased her pace a little. 'I'm in no hurry,' she shrugged.

The stifled expletive that ensued was definitely nearer, but just how near she didn't realise until she was abruptly spun around to face him. 'Okay, so what's been bugging you all evening, hmm?' he demanded on an exasperated note.

Devon took a step backwards, her eyes flashing with a militant light, her breathing quickening uncontrollably. How dared he stand there acting as if *she* had something to answer for, when in actual fact it should have been just the opposite!

'For a start, your continuing interference in my family's affairs!' she exploded tempestuously. 'I told you the other night why Dad shouldn't be considering that trip!'

'And I told you why I thought he should!'

'That doesn't make it your business to be encouraging him to. . .'

'He asked for my opinion, and I gave it!' he interrupted peremptorily.

She rounded her eyes sarcastically. 'And why would your opinion suddenly be so important to him?'

'Maybe because he knows his self-absorbed daughter's would be too biased!' he shot back in unsparing tones.

Her chin started to tremble and she clenched her jaw resolutely to stop it. 'In that case, I wonder why he invited me to go with him, then!'

'And are you?' Hunt probed watchfully instead of replying.

'How could I?' she flared. 'I've got a fiancé to consider too, remember?' Halting, she sent him an acrimonious glare before going on bitterly, 'But of course you do! After all, discussions concerning Garth and myself are apparently nothing new for you and your latest girlfriend! What do you do, give her a rundown on each day's proceedings so you can laugh about it together? That m-must really top off y-your evenings!' Her voice began to break and she swallowed painfully. 'Or perhaps that's when your unwanted pity comes to the fore, is it? That is, if it's possible for anyone as utterly ruthless and contemptible as you to even know the meaning of the word!' Now an ungovernable sob did force its way out, and with her eyes misting treacherously she took to her heels.

It appeared Hunt didn't see that as the end of the matter as she did, however, for within a few strides he was level with her again. Wanting only to escape him, Devon swerved and raced for the dunes, an action which immediately proved to be a mistake as her foot caught in one of the creepers and she went sprawling to the ground. Hunt promptly sank down on to his haunches beside her, but when she would have scrambled to her feet again a hand catching hold of her ankle had her collapsing unceremoniously once more. A hold that was then exchanged for one around her wrist, which accordingly guaranteed any other attempts to flee were out of the question.

'Now perhaps you'd care to tell me just what the hell that was all about!' he suggested at his satirically mocking best.

Nor surprisingly, it wasn't an approach that appealed to his captive. 'As if you don't know! But that's all you like to do, isn't it, Hunt? Make fun of people!' she charged, striking out at him with her free hand.

In next to no time that wrist was securely imprisoned too, and as he also lowered himself into a sitting position, he pulled her around so that she was at right angles to him.

'No, not all,' he refuted finally, but with some subtle nuance evident that had a slight nervousness mingling with her rancour. 'Right at present I can think of a number of things I'd like to do to you, sweetheart, believe me! And quite possibly might . . . if I don't soon get some answers!'

'I thought that was purely your domain!' she dared to gibe heedlessly. 'You surely don't expect me—the naïve misfit you apparently can't figure out, so in your patronising arrogance you decide to pity instead—to have anything to say that would be of interest to you!'

'Yes, that's exactly what I'm expecting!' he asserted roughly, his brows snapping together in a frown. 'Because I only wish to God I knew what on earth you're talking about with all this "naïve misfit" and "pity" rubbish!'

'Is it?' Devon attempted to counter in derisive disbelief but was unable to prevent an edge of despondency from creeping in. 'Your girlfriend tells a different story!'

'Well, that's enlightening, to say the least!' he retorted, caustically dry. 'I wasn't even aware I had a girlfriend!'

'Oh? Then what else would you call someone you've evidently been almost inseparable from ever since you arrived?'

To her anguish, he laughed at that. 'Sweetheart, if you cast your mind back, I believe you'll find the only person I've been almost inseparable from since I arrived is *you!*' he pointed out wryly. 'Although somehow I get the feeling that's not who you were meaning.'

'As you very well know!' she retorted resentfully, although in a somewhat more moderate fashion now that she understood the reason for his amusement. 'We're talking about Pauline!' Her tone began to strengthen again. 'You know, the girl you like to discuss—ridicule, more like—Garth and myself with.'

'Do I?' His brows peaked graphically in unison. 'That's the first I've heard of it.'

'Well, it obviously isn't for her! And if you weren't discussing us, then why would she be explaining anything about me to you?'

'Oh, yeah, I remember now,' he drawled on an ironic note that did nothing to appease her smouldering feelings. 'I asked her if you'd ever dated any of the yachtsmen who called in here. She said, no, not to her knowledge. End of conversation!' One corner of his mouth lifted with mocking eloquence. 'Big discussion!'

Devon gazed at him dubiously. 'Pauline implied differently,' she put forward, but in somewhat less assured tones.

'And because I'm automatically on trial every time I

open my bloody mouth, you believe her unquestion-
ingly, of course!' For only the second time since she
had known him there was a decided sting in Hunt's
voice. 'And that, despite the fact that, any idea of
yours to the contrary, I've hardly spoken to the girl
more than half a dozen times, and then usually only
briefly!'

'I—well—she's got no reason to lie!' Devon
abruptly found herself on the defensive.

'And I have?'

The hard deliberation with which the question was
delivered had her stirring discomfitedly. She supposed
not, and yet . . . 'Well, you certainly appear to be on—
er—very close terms with her! Every time you were
together back there,' nodding towards the clearing,
'you had your arm round her!' she recalled tartly, and
a trifle reproachfully too, she noted in gathering
dismay.

Hunt flexed a broad shoulder dismissively. 'The
way Pauline inserts herself beside you, it's difficult to
do anything else.'

'And is that also why she's been out to the
*Kanandah* so often?' She pulled a disbelieving face.

'I wouldn't know.' He shrugged again. 'I've only
been aboard once when she's been out there.'

That once having been sufficiently satisfactory,
though, from Pauline's viewpoint! 'How disappointing
for you!' she couldn't restrain from gibing, then
immediately wished she hadn't on seeing the shrewdly
speculative look that came over his face.

'Oh? What makes you say that?' His head tilted
lazily and he ran a disturbing finger along the fragile
line of her jaw. 'And in such an—umm—accusing
fashion too!'

'Accusing!' she just managed to get out with an appropriately humorous tinkle of laughter. 'Don't be ridiculous! Why should I care what the two of you do?'

'That's what I wonder . . . because you do seem to be dwelling on the matter, don't you, sweetheart?'

'O-only in order to discover who's telling the truth! And—and only in so far as it concerns myself, of course,' she added hastily, judiciously.

Leaning forward slightly, Hunt slid his hands slowly up her arms and across her shoulders to cup her head securely. 'Then perhaps this will help make up your mind,' he proposed softly as his head lowered to hers.

It wasn't hard to divine his intention and Devon strained frantically away from the touch she knew could turn her bones to liquid and what little defence she did possess into a disquieting, unconditional capitulation. 'No! Stop it! That proves nothing!' she contended desperately.

'It does to me.'

But what? That she could no more resist him than could Pauline? The humiliating thought gave her the stimulus to remind, albeit with a jerky breathlessness, 'Be-besides, there's G-Garth.'

'So?' Hunt enquired with indolent indifference against her quivering lips.

She swallowed despairingly, guiltily. 'He is my f-fiancé, after all.'

'Then maybe he shouldn't be!' came the disconcerting opinion, and with none of the irresolution she had evinced, as his mouth finally, sensuously claimed hers.

No, maybe he shouldn't, Devon was forced into conceding on finding the hands that had been meant to be pushing at Hunt were instead spontaneously linking about his neck, and her lips responding unreservedly to his tantalising possession of them. Not while another man was capable of making her forget everything but himself and awakening such potent feelings within her as this man could, and was doing—and as Garth never had.

With her lips willingly returning the demanding pressure of his, Devon swayed towards Hunt's virile frame unknowingly, and offered no resistance when his encircling arms drew her down beside him on the sand. His mouth was warm and compelling as it moved with unhurried thoroughness from her lips to her throat, her shoulder, and back to her eagerly waiting mouth again; his hands strong but gentle as they traced her curving form; the hard male shape of him stimulating as it pressed against her invitingly pliant body.

Gaining courage, Devon slid her hands under the silk knit of his shirt, feeling the corded muscles of his back tense beneath the experimental play of her fingers. She had never touched a man in such a fashion before and the emotions it galvanised into life were entirely new to her too. As were those that soon after had her pulse racing erratically and her breath coming in ragged gasps when first Hunt's hands and then his stirring mouth found and explored the rounded contours and throbbing nipples of her sun-gilded breasts.

With a groan, Hunt clasped her to him even more tightly, his fingers tangling amidst the silken strands of her tousled, golden hair as his mouth sought hers one last fevered time. 'Oh, God, you could drive a man to distraction!' he declared huskily against her parted lips. 'Much more of this and you won't have any innocence left at all.' His lips twisted ruefully. 'You learn too fast, I'm afraid, little sea nymph.'

Still floundering in a sea of newly rioting emotions, Devon flushed self-consciously. In other words, she had shown herself too willing, too uninhibited, she deduced, cringing inwardly at the humiliating thought. Obviously he hadn't minded indulging in a few harmless kisses, but just as evidently he hadn't anticipated, or wanted, it progressing any further. Easing away from him she dragged her top back into place embarrassedly.

'I'm sorry,' she offered stiffly, her features held no less tautly as she attempted to disguise her feelings of shame.

Hunt gazed at her strangely. 'For what, for crying out loud?'

Saved the added mortification of answering by a familiar female voice suddenly calling, 'Hunt! Hunt, where are you? It's unkind of you to disappear like this. You know you're the only one I like dancing with. We fit together . . .' there was an expressive pause, 'so cosily.' Devon took the opportunity to gain her feet with alacrity.

'It would appear your girlfriend feels deserted,' she sniped bitterly.

In a matter of seconds Hunt was on his own feet. 'And I told you, I don't *have* a girlfriend!' he denied on a rough note.

'No, it doesn't sound like it!' she scorned and, just managing to evade the arm he flung out to stop her, fled between two bushes of sea lettuce just before Pauline made her appearance via the beach.

By the time Devon had cut through to the path

leading up to the house her cheeks were wet with tears of pain and abasement. Tears that were still falling when she reached the safety of her bedroom. Never, *never*, would she allow him to make her feel so degraded again! she promised herself vehemently.

# CHAPTER SEVEN

DURING the next couple of days Devon kept herself as busy as possible at the house, ostensibly to help her aunt prepare for their coming influx of Eastern personnel, but also in the hope of avoiding giving herself time to think, as much as anything. Nevertheless, the frequent sight of her father, Royce and Hunt either checking certain aspects of the island's equipment, or else just merely conversing, made it very difficult for her to exclude Hunt from her mind completely for any length of time, and particularly when, after seeing him return to the *Kanandah* each day, she made her way down to Careen Beach for her usual swim.

Then she found it almost impossible to keep him out of her thoughts at all. Perhaps because the beach continually reminded her of the one occasion when they had seemed to be in total harmony, she reasoned pensively. Although that really didn't satisfactorily explain just why she should also find herself, despite all her motives for not doing so, missing his mostly aggravating presence to quite such an extent, the perturbing thought usually ensued.

Because miss him she certainly did, she finally had to admit, even if only to herself and with the greatest reluctance. The same as she had to concede, after many days spent desperately fighting the notion, that she also missed those arousing kisses he had bestowed on her daily and which, subconsciously at least, she grudgingly acknowledged, she had eventually come to expect. The reason why she should miss them, though, wasn't one she cared to delve into too deeply, however. It was sufficiently discomposing, not to say alarming, to discover she missed them at all!

Hunt, on the other hand, didn't appear to miss her company in the slightest. In fact, he gave the appearance of being quite content with matters as they were, treating her with a casualness that probably troubled her all the more due to its sheer nonchalance, on those rare occasions when they did accidentally meet, although without any diminishing of his customary mockery, she noted, but definitely without displaying even the smallest desire to spend any time alone with her again. A circumstance that only added weight to her supposition that he had merely been amusing himself previously, first by seeking to prove she was no more immune to his indisputably proficient brand of love-making than any other female probably was, and then by making her feel an abandoned wanton once he had succeeded in his aim.

No less depressing either, Devon discovered, was that his last thought-provoking remark concerning her fiancé also refused to be dispelled from her mind so that, as a result, when Garth did manage to get out to the island on a locally owned yacht for a few days, she greeted him with an enthusiasm and demonstrativeness that hadn't characterised their relationship before in an attempt to prove that he was as capable of stimulating the same fervent feelings within her as Hunt was.

When he not only didn't, but also remonstrated in a somewhat annoyed tone, 'For heaven's sake, Devon, I hardly think it's necessary for you to be quite so—so unrestrained! After all, I've only been away for a couple of days, and when all's said and done, I don't really consider it's very feminine of you to make your feelings known in such a fashion. I've always believed that to be the man's sole prerogative!' she had no choice but to dismally accede that he wasn't the man for her as she had previously believed.

At the same time, however, and against everything that told her it was only fair that she advise Garth of her decision immediately, she still had no intention of actually breaking their engagement and returning his ring while Hunt was still on the island. The idea that he would promptly deduce, correctly as it might be, that he had been the cause of such an action and thereby doubtlessly provide him with even more humorous satisfaction, was just too humiliating to contemplate, and so she did her best to portray the role of one entirely complacent with their lot during the remainder of her fiancé's stay.

The day after Garth's departure the *Coral Trader* arrived again, this time with Hunt's staff aboard together with all their equipment, including a water drilling rig—something Devon's father had also often thought of having shipped out to the island, but the cost had always been beyond him. Apparently, though, Hunt was of the same idea as he was, that as with the Great Artesian Basin which covered over a million square miles of the mainland, after millenia of such high rainfall as the north received there was more than likely a good chance that somewhere beneath Cowrie there was an even greater intake bed than the one at present yielding the island's comparatively unsubstantial water supply.

Not surprisingly, Violet was in her element with so

many more, and appreciative, mouths to feed, and after the first few days even Devon lost most of her antagonism towards them in the face of their affable and often hilarious company. Not that she saw much of any of them during the day, but with the evening meal their good-natured bantering, from which neither she, her father and aunt, nor their two remaining guests were allowed to escape, would invariably begin so that by the end of the first week it seemed as if they had all known each other for years instead of merely days.

The only fly in the ointment Devon could see was that two days after the men's arrival—and coincidental with the day that Pauline Telfer and her brother departed in their yacht, she noted caustically—Hunt and Royce also moved into the guesthouse in order to both be on site as the investigations proceeded, as well as because the massive dining table provided far greater space and convenience for their nightly reviews and discussions. It wasn't an arrangement that suited Devon at all, and for the hundredth time wished her father wasn't so damned accommodating where the younger man was concerned, because it was he who had suggested the move!

In the middle of the following week the drilling rig struck the water they had been searching for so diligently, and at a flow rate that predicted Cowrie would never again be subject to a shortage of that precious commodity no matter how many people stayed on the island. Naturally enough, for all those connected with the company it was a result to be celebrated, but not for Devon because she somehow knew that nothing would stop the sale taking place now. Nevertheless, throughout the meal that evening she did her best to keep her disconsolate feelings from showing, particularly when she became aware of Hunt's eyes fixed intently upon her as they so often had in the past. Whatever happened, she wasn't going to provide him with any more gratification by revealing just how despondent she actually was.

Not even after serving everyone else's coffee in the sitting room—their usual nightly conference presumably having been waived due to the day's events—and she took Hunt's in to the dining room where he was perusing a pile of sketches and papers alone did she betray by so much as a change of expression how the discovery had affected her.

For his part, Hunt watched her deposit the cup on the table with the same absorbed gaze that had been present during the meal, but then, as she turned to leave caught hold of her wrist in a loose grip momentarily—just long enough to bring her to a halt—whereupon he immediately released it again.

'I'm sorry,' he said quietly, unexpectedly, his glance unwavering. 'You know what today's discovery means, don't you?'

'That Cowrie will now definitely change hands?' With her features tightly controlled, she nodded. Then, accompanied by a suitably deprecating shrug, 'Oh, well, as has been said before, I guess all good things have to end sometime, don't they? I daresay I'll survive.'

'Even without the extra your fiancé tried angling for?'

Now her demeanour did alter. To one of total bewilderment. 'I don't know what you're talking about. What extra?' she frowned in confusion.

'The additional sum he wanted added to the purchase price which, he assured us, would enable him to guarantee your full co-operation in future,' he divulged bluntly.

'Oh!' Astonishment had Devon sinking on to the chair next to him as his completely unanticipated revelation seemed to reverberate within her head. Suddenly her eyes narrowed and she looked at him sharply. 'You said . . . us? Are you saying you have a witness to this—this supposed proposition?'

Hunt's mouth shaped sardonically. 'Still as doubtful as ever, eh, sweetheart?' he charged. 'But yes, I have a witness . . . Royce, as a matter of fact.' He paused, significantly. 'Plus a tape recording of the whole miserable conversation, as it so happens. When he came out to the *Kanandah* wanting to see me the last time he was here, I thought it could be interesting to have a copy of what he had to say.'

Devon's hopes plummeted, and in their stead came indignation. Even without a tape recording she wouldn't have doubted a confirmation from Royce. He had always struck her as being extremely honest and above board. But that Garth should have had the hide to take it on himself to try and extort, there really wasn't any other word for it, more money from them was absolutely insupportable! And if she had wanted any further reason for convincing herself she was doing the right thing in intending to break their engagement, this was well and truly it! But by having mentioned her, did that also mean. . .

'But you surely don't believe I had anything to do with that, do you?' she gasped. 'I mean, why would I be asking for more money? I don't even know what you offered in the first place!'

His head angled in a manner she could only call sceptical. 'Don't you?'

'No!' she almost shouted. Inexplicably, it was suddenly very important that she convince him of that, as well as having had nothing whatsoever to do with Garth's conniving. 'Just ask Dad if you don't believe me! He can tell you I wasn't interested in knowing! The same as I told Garth I wasn't when he found out what your offer was!' Halting, her head drooped and her voice became huskier. 'I was only ever interested in retaining Cowrie, not in how much we were likely to get for it.'

'As I suspected when Wilkinson came to see us,' Hunt disclosed on a somewhat wry note. He uttered a short, humorless laugh. 'What I didn't expect, though, was that you were *so* against the sale that you didn't even want to know that much about it.'

'But you do believe I had nothing to do with Garth going to see you?' She reached out a tentatively pleading hand, then promptly retracted it before it could actually touch his arm.

'Yeah, well, maybe my judgment of human character is a little better than yours, because I had strong doubts right from the start regarding your likely involvement,' he drawled, not a little mockingly, and had her cheeks colouring in consequence.

It was the second time he had insinuated as much, and because he apparently hadn't believed she'd been a party to Garth's ploy, she now found herself feeling guilty for having suspected him of inventing the story.

'I'm sorry,' it was her turn to apologise now, dolefully. 'It was just that it came as such a shock, and on top of—on top of. . .' She faltered to a stop, trying frantically to regain her earlier expressionless manner.

For a minute or two silence reigned until Hunt broke it with an almost musing, 'I know you said you didn't want to work here if the sale took place, but have you ever considered at least remaining until the resort is ready to open? After all, the constructions crews, etcetera, will all have to be fed and taken care of and not even your aunt, as capable as she obviously is, could manage that without any help. I imagine she'll need at least another two, if not three, to help her, and I'm sure she'd much prefer it if you were one of them, especially as you do already know the ropes here.'

Aquamarine eyes flickered in surprise. 'You're offering me a job?' she sounded cautiously.

'Again,' his concurrence was drily given.

Devon's first thought was to refuse, outright, just as she had before, but then an almost defiant reasoning began to prevail. It was true, her aunt *would* require help, so why shouldn't she be one of those to provide it? Besides, as he had deduced, Aunt Violet would no doubt prefer it if she stayed, she told herself bracingly.

'All right, then for Aunt Violet's sake I will stay on . . . until the resort goes into operation,' she added the last hurriedly, just so he wouldn't think she was having second thoughts about her prior decision as well. 'Th-thank you.' It was an effort to get the words out but she supposed she owed him that much at least.

In response, Hunt's lips quirked expressively, as if well aware of her thought processes. 'Okay, I'll get Royce to advise the appropriate people within the company,' was all he said though.

Devon nodded her acknowledgment faintly and began to rise. She was pleased her time on the island had been extended, and yet, conversely, she was unsure now whether she had actually made the right decision.

Meanwhile, Hunt gathered up some of the sketches on the table. 'Would you like to see some of Clive's preliminary drawings before you go?' he suddenly looked up to enquire.

Once again, her initial thought was to decline, but unaccountably she found herself sitting again without consciously realising she was doing so. 'I guess so,' she shrugged, deciding that now she was re-seated she may as well, and accepted the sheaf of papers he handed her.

Clive Bassett was the company's architect and it didn't take her long to acknowledge, even if reluctantly, that he was obviously not only an able one but an extremely imaginative one also. Although the drawings were only in the rough, they depicted a variety of designs and layouts for the proposed resort, and even at that stage it was clear to see that the buildings were intended to blend in with their surroundings rather than dominate them. One sketch in particular caught her interest and after studying it for a few minutes her mouth began to curve wistfully.

'I like the general idea of that one,' she finally said impulsively. Actually, she hadn't meant to comment on any of them but the words just seemed to slip out of their own volition.

'Because it incorporates the house?' Hunt hazarded wryly.

'Probably,' she shrugged again, not wanting to discuss it further. The whole idea was still too new for her to be able to accept it with complete indifference. Fortunately, an abrupt pounding on the roof acted as a diversion and her expression took on a whimsical cast. 'What with today's discovery, and now this, it would appear you'll very shortly have more water than you know what to do with.'

Listening to the thunder of the rain, Hunt's brows rose quizzically. 'You're saying the wet's begun ... already?'

Tempted to endorse the assumption—it was evident there was still an amount of groundwork he wished completed before the rain did arrive in earnest—she eventually decided against it. The weather itself would soon disprove it, anyway.

'Not quite,' she therefore disclosed. 'It's just the first of our nightly deluges that come as a prelude. It'll be fine again by morning. Just distinctly more humid, that's all.'

'A comforting thought,' he immediately quipped on a rueful note, but obviously relieved all the same. Then, after a slight pause, 'While on the subject of drawings, though ... I hear from Matt that you've been doing some that could be suitable as a logo for the island.'

Devon shook her head vehemently, railing yet once more against her parent's loquaciousness. Wasn't there *anything* he didn't intend to disclose to this man? 'Not really,' she denied tautly. 'I was simply trying some new designs one time and they happened to be of shells, that's all.'

'Cowrie shells?'

'Well—yes—but they're nothing out of the ordinary.'

'Matt seemed to think they were some of the best you'd ever done,' he persisted.

Thanks Dad! she grimaced silently, tartly. 'Even if they are, they're still my property to do with as I see fit,' she opted to challenge instead of defend now.

'True,' he allowed, nodding. 'But since we want a logo, and you've apparently designed one that could be acceptable, don't you think it's a little petty, just because matters haven't turned out as you wanted, for us not to come to some arrangement?'

'Not particularly!' She eyed him rancorously. So now she was petty just because she wouldn't fall in with his wishes, was she? 'In any case, as far as I'm concerned one member of this family coming to an arrangement with you has been more than sufficient!'

'An arrangement, I might point out, however, that hasn't exactly been to your disadvantage!' Hunt retorted, his voice sharpening no less than hers.

'Monetary-wise, maybe!' she granted on a jeering note. 'But what's the use of money when, to get it, you have to sell the very thing you wanted to keep? That sort of defeats the purpose, doesn't it?'

'Except that Matt, as the owner, obviously *did* want to sell!'

His pungent reminder, as always, had her subsiding defeatedly, leaving her feeling empty inside. 'So he did,' she acceded in low, self-mocking tones. 'Your good luck, my bad, it would appear.' And in the same despondently flippant accents as she rose to her feet for the second time, 'Accordingly, I suppose there's no reason for you not to have my drawings either, is there? Especially since you've made me realise how meaningless it would be for me to keep them.' She turned for the doorway leading to the hall. 'I'll get them for you now.'

'Devon . . . for God's sake!' she heard him exclaim roughly behind her, but just kept walking. That was, until her ears also picked up the sound of his chair being thrust back, whereupon her pace increased markedly.

As it was, she reached her room only mere seconds in front of him, and before she could close the door behind her he had pushed peremptorily inside.

'I said I'd get them for you, Hunt! I didn't say you were welcome to come and collect them!' she immediatly gritted.

'aMybe not, but then I wasn't expecting you to react like you just did either! And believe it or not . . .' a captivatingly wry smile began playing about the edges of his attractive mouth, 'I was worried about you.'

Devon swallowed hard as a mute sob rose in her throat. Not so much as a result of what he'd said, but the realisation that if he had beckoned to her at that moment she knew she would willingly have fallen into his arms. Oh, God, what was the matter with her that she allowed him to have such an overwhelming effect on her, particularly after all he'd done? she despaired.

'Oh, I see, so to add to selfish and petty and all the other uncomplimentary adjectives you've described me with, you're now inferring I'm unbalanced too, are you?' she gibed. If her head couldn't rule her emotions where he was concerned, it did at least still have control of her words. 'Well, for your information, Hunter Kincaid, I can assure you you're way off beam because it would take a great deal more than anything you can throw at me to reduce me to that state!' Forcing out a faintly hysterical tinkle of amused laughter she moved across to her desk and picked up a folder which she held out to him. 'Call them a parting gift, if you like. In the hope we never meet again!'

Although he took the folder from her, it was only in order to throw it on to her bed. 'No, thanks! I don't need you doing me any favours, you perverse, petulant little bitch!' Hunt rasped, his eyes snapping with a steely blue fire she had never seen before. 'No matter how good they may or may not be, I wouldn't touch them now if you paid me! Thankfully, no one's irreplaceable, not even you, sweetheart,' witheringly, rather than endearingly, 'so I doubt I'll have any difficulty in finding someone else capable of designing a logo equally as good as, if not better than, any of yours! I merely thought you may have liked to know that something of yourself would be remaining on Cowrie even after you'd left!' He dipped his dark head mockingly, derisively, as he opened the door. 'Sorry! It appears my judgment—regarding you, at least— isn't as accurate as I believed—trusted—it to be!' And before she could even open her mouth he had gone, the door shutting with resounding finality behind him.

For a time Devon stood motionless, staring at the position where he had last been, her eyes blurring uncontrollably. She supposed she should have been happy—after all, it appeared she'd finally succeeded in really putting that distance between them that she'd always wanted—but unpredictably she wasn't. She was the most miserable and confused she had ever been in her life and, with a choking cry, she tossed her folder of drawings on to the floor carelessly before throwing herself on the bed in their place, her tears starting to fall at a rate that matched the rain continuing to drum overhead.

Three weeks later, without there having been more than a dozen cool sentences exchanged between them, Devon watched with an ache in the pit of her stomach as Hunt departed on the *Kanandah* one wet and windy, though still warm day. The rest of the company's personnel had

left on the launch the day before, so that now she stood
all alone on the verandah—her father having accepted
Hunt's offer to take him to Northport in order that the
appropriate papers connected with the island's sale
might be signed and a deposit paid; her aunt deciding to
take the opportunity to accompany them and have
something of a holiday while she was still able—the tears
that had kept appearing for no apparent reason during
the last few weeks once again spilling over her thick
lashes to mingle with the rain the wind was blowing
unheeded on to her cheeks.

Brushing them away with the backs of her fingers
she tried to concentrate on what needed to be done
around the place while her father and aunt were away,
but it was impossible to do while her eyes steadfastly
refused to waver for one instant from the white-hulled
boat now receding swiftly into the distance. Not even
after it had finally disappeared from sight altogether
did she immediately move, because it was only in
those last few seconds, knowing it was unlikely she
would ever see Hunt again, that she realised she was
watching his departure so tenaciously, so anguishedly,
due to her loving him with all her heart and soul and
actually not wanting him to leave at all!

Now she could at least understand why he had come
to have such an overpowering effect on her emotions,
even if she did find it difficult to accept. After all,
she'd instinctively known right from the beginning
that he spelt danger for any female unthinking enough
to become involved with him, and if his association
with Pauline hadn't endorsed that conviction and
made her doubly wary, then his own quite open
comment about promises to marry never having been
in his line certainly should have.

That they evidently hadn't was more than óbvious now, though, and wiping her fingers across her eyes again she turned and made her way cheerlessly inside the house. It wasn't the first time she'd had the island all to herself—quite often when the guesthouse experienced a slack period they would all take it in turns to spend some time on the mainland—but whereas she usually enjoyed the solitude, on this occasion, with nothing to distract her thoughts, she suspected it was going to be intolerably dismal.

As it happened, however, her mind became fully occupied with other, more pressing, matters during the next couple of days because as the wind progressively strengthened, the rain increased, and the barometric pressure steadily dropped, Devon soon began to suspect that something a little more impressive than a mere wet spell may have been forming somewhere to the north. A suspicion that was proved correct when she put a radio telephone call through to her father on the mainland.

That he was also very concerned about being unable to return due to the conditions brought about by that apparent cyclone was obvious too, but after assuring him she knew exactly what to do, and ascertaining the route it was predicted it might take—accurately forecasting the likely direction something as wholly unpredictable as a cyclone might take was an impossibility; sometimes they would meander up and down the coast for a few days before either turning out to sea and dissipating, as the majority of them thankfully did, or else suddenly descending on the mainland, with devastating effect on occasion—she did her utmost to put his mind at rest regarding her safety before ringing off and setting about making her preparations.

By early afternoon Devon was satisfied she had taken every precaution she could, as she explained to her father when he phoned to advise that Cyclone Muriel, now rated important enough to warrant its own name, had definitely started moving southwards and that although not expected, at that stage, to pass directly over Cowrie, its path still wouldn't be all that far distant. A deduction Devon had already made for herself actually because the force of the wind and rain had been increasing drastically hour by hour, and as she surmised they must have been doing all day in Northport too when their line suddenly went dead. Now she really was on her own, she thought ruefully, and hurriedly had a shower and then cooked herself an early dinner while she could still do so before venturing outside in order to turn off the generators and pump—just in case.

Just how much more savage were the elements now Devon promptly realised as she literally had to struggle against the wind that tore at her clothes, while the rain beating so ferociously into her face made it difficult to see and therefore avoid the palm leaves and other assorted natural debris that was being wrested from the already violently buffeted vegetation. Grateful for the brief respite while inside the machine sheds, she delayed her return a moment as she looked out to sea from the doorway. This was very definitely one of those times when the Pacific made a mockery of its name, she thought drily, for now it was a heaving, churning, maelstrom of water that exploded against the reef in mountainous spray-scattering waves that had already filled the lagoon well past its normal high-water mark. Happily, Devon knew the ground the house was situated upon was high enough to escape any storm surge that might occur, but even so it was still rather unsettling to see the normally placid waters of the lagoon pounding furiously higher and higher along the foreshores.

By midnight the wind was a howling, shrieking fiend, the rain such a deafening crescendo on the roof that it completely drowned out the sounds of destruction Devon knew must be occurring outside. The house itself she didn't really have too many worries about. In its seventy-odd years of life it had successfully withstood a number of such storms, and although it was high-set the steel bolts fixing it to its concrete stumps were specifically designed to ensure it couldn't be blown off its foundations, while those securing the roof helped guarantee that wasn't likely to abruptly disappear either.

An hour later her ears, attuned as they were to the noise now, told her that the worst was over and that it had definitely begun to ease; another hour after that and she knew it had moved even further away from the island, and with a thankful sigh she was finally able to retire to her bed.

# CHAPTER EIGHT

WHEN she awoke Devon lay still for a moment, hardly able to credit the comparative silence that greeted her. There was only a slight breeze she could hear outside, certainly no rain, and not only that but through her shuttered bedroom windows she thought she could even detect what seemed to be faint flickerings of sunlight. Rolling to her feet she hurried down the hall and threw open the back door, staring in shocked dismay at the view that met her eyes.

The vegetation had been decimated. Trees uprooted, some merely sheered off halfway, while those that had been left standing were completely stripped of most of their branches, together with all their leaves, as had the majority of the other shrubs and bushes about the place. With nothing to impede her vision now, she could also see that one of the outbuildings had lost some sheets of iron from its roof, one of which was deeply embedded in a corner post of the verandah. A quick inspection of the house as she opened the shutters thankfully showed that to be the only damage it appeared to have suffered, though, and with a last eloquent grimace for the clearing up that was ahead of her she returned inside to wash and have something to eat before starting to tackle it.

Half an hour later she was back on the verandah again, shading her eyes against the bright, though still rather overcast sky as the sound of an approaching helicopter broke the stillness. Initially, she thought it

must have been one of the emergency services aircraft
checking the area, but as it drew closer she could see
no such easily identifiable markings and wondered
what on earth anyone else would be doing out that
way. When it became evident it intended landing she
was even more surprised—she couldn't even remember
one setting down on Cowrie before—and waited
curiously as the machine was efficiently brought to
rest on the lawn at the back of the house.

A man's tall form, clad in slim fitting jeans and a
maroon T-shirt, emerged almost immediately and
Devon's breath caught in her throat as she instantly
recognised him. In fact, she even took a couple of
involuntary steps down the stairs, but then brought
herself to a determined halt. Although her heart was
racing ecstatically at the sight of him, she knew that if
she wanted to retain any of her pride and self-respect
at all she could never allow such feelings to show.
Accordingly, when Hunt reached the bottom of the
steps her expression was carefully schooled.

'Come to check how your assets have fared, have
you?' she gibed sardonically.

'Not especially,' he disclaimed, flexing an impassive
shoulder. 'Unlike some, I've always considered people
more important than property.' His eyes abruptly
lifted to hers and held. 'You're all okay?'

Against her will she found herself responding to the
concern in his voice and some of her deliberate
antagonism receded. 'Well, I expect Dad and Aunt
Violet are. They're still in Northport. The telephone
went out yesterday afternoon and I haven't been able
to contact them since,' she revealed matter-of-factly.

'You're saying, you were here all on your own last
night?' he frowned.

She gave a deprecating shrug. 'Dad wanted to get back, but he couldn't because of the weather. It just came up too quickly.'

'Hell! It never occurred to me that you might still be alone here.' Pausing, he eyed her closely. 'That couldn't have been very pleasant for you.'

'Maybe a little unnerving,' she admitted on a wry note. 'But the house is really as good as cyclone proof these days so I wasn't too worried.' A rueful curve caught at her lips. 'Well, most of the time I wasn't.'

His answering smile of understanding played havoc with her emotions and in an effort to both hide the effect as well as overcome it, she went on swiftly. 'So who else caught it besides Cowrie? Do you know?'

'Oh, Northport to some degree, of course, plus a couple of smaller towns down the coast, but it hasn't actually moved ashore as yet. It's still travelling southwards.'

'They usually do,' she nodded.

'I can't say I'm sorry,' he half smiled expressively, looking at the devastation surrounding them. 'My God, the place looks as if a bomb's hit it!' He began mounting the steps, his mouth shaping with lazy mockery. 'Something else you forgot to mention happens around here?'

'I—well. . .' she began flusteredly as she backed away slightly. 'You must have known this was a cyclone area, and—and it's not as if this sort of thing happens every year. We may normally get a storm or two during the season, but something like this only occurs once in every twenty years or more.' Recovered now, she sent him a not altogether unhopeful glance from beneath long, curling lashes. 'However, if you're having second thoughts about buying the place. . .'

'Uh-uh!' Hunt broke in with a laconic but drily decisive negation. 'The deal stands. Granted, I didn't expect to see it ravaged in quite such a fashion within a week of purchasing it, but simultaneously, it's not entirely a bad thing to have had happen. I've now seen it under its best and worst conditions and that can only assist us with our planning.'

Pulling only a lightly grimacing face—subconsciously she didn't really think she'd been expecting otherwise—she shrugged, 'You'll be wanting to see all over the place again, then, I suppose?'

He didn't actually confirm it, but countered banteringly instead, 'Is that an offer to be my guide once more?'

'No!' she ejaculated in patent dismay. Feeling as she did about him, the last thing she wanted was to be alone with him for any length of time. She would be bound to give herself away. 'You know the island well enough now not to need a guide.'

'Couldn't handle it twice, huh?'

No, she couldn't, but for entirely different reasons than he supposed. At least, she sincerely hoped they were different reasons! 'Whether I could or not has nothing to do with it,' she claimed, trying to inject some firmness into her voice. 'There's simply too much to be done here, as you can see,' with an expressively outspread hand, 'for me to waste time traipsing all over the place.'

Before her hand could drop to her side again, Hunt caught hold of it. 'I also see you're not wearing your engagement ring,' he drawled. 'Why's that?'

With a gulp, Devon dragged her fingers free immediately, clasping them with her other hand as if by hiding the bare untanned mark the ring had left she could deny its telltale presence. 'B-because I took it off, of course,' she quipped shakily, protectively. As she had always intended to do as soon as he'd left. 'It—it kept catching on things while I was working yesterday.'

His intensely blue eyes roamed over her indolently, disturbingly. 'So you're still planning to marry him?'

'Naturally,' she just managed to push out in something like a normal tone. 'There's no reason why I shouldn't.'

'Except that you don't happen to love him?'

The noticeable irony in his remark had her stiffening resentfully. 'No? And what would you know about it? There's more to love than mere physical attraction or—or compatibility, you know!'

'You don't say!' he mocked. 'But you sure as hell can't have a full and satisfying relationship without it . . . as you very well know, only you're too damned frightened to admit it!'

'Frightened!' she expostulated in a passably scoffing manner. 'Why should I be frightened to admit anything, *if* I believed it was the truth?'

He took a step closer, his firmly moulded mouth shaping wryly. 'In case you inadvertently betray how you really feel.'

Devon moistened her lips nervously as she promptly increased the distance between them again. 'I've just t-told you that,' she stammered.

'Mmm, I know what you *told* me, but. . .'

'Well, then,' she interposed swiftly with a shrug as if that settled the matter. And desperate to change the subject, 'So now, why don't you have your look round, and let me start on what needs to be done here?' She made to step past him and head down the steps.

'Uh-uh!' No sooner had she begun to move than an arm reaching across to the stair rail was barring her way. 'That can wait. That's not why I flew all the way out here.'

Devon gave up attempting to push his arm away in order to stare up at him with eyes bright with unshed, and inexplicable tears. 'Then apart from checking out the island, what is? Just so you can taunt me about my engagement again? Well, thanks all the same but right at the moment I don't need it! I didn't exactly have an enjoyable time last night, and. . .'

'You think I did?' Hunt clasped her by the shoulders, shaking her. 'Knowing you were out here while that tempest was raging, and not being able to do a damned thing about it! God! Maybe it was just as well I didn't know you were here alone . . . otherwise I don't know what I would have done! Gone off my head completely, probably!' Releasing her abruptly, he swung away raking a hand savagely through the thickness of his hair, then turned back with a rueful shake of his head. 'I know you've never trusted me, but you don't even trust yourself, do you, sweetheart?'

Still trying to assimilate the incredible fact that he had apparently been worried on *her* account, Devon could only proffer a tremulously confused, 'I don't know what you mean.'

'I mean, just for once, try believing in your own feelings,' he enlightened her on a resonant note as he brushed his hand against her cheek gently. 'Do you think I don't know why you were crying when the *Kanandah* left?'

'Who—who says I was?' she parried jerkily, blinking in her surprise.

'I do . . . with the aid of a pair of binoculars.'

'Oh!' She averted her gaze in consternation. 'It could just have been—been the rain.'

His lips twisted wryly. 'Except we both know it wasn't. Besides, do you always watch people you dislike until they're out of sight? In those circumstances most others wouldn't have bothered to watch at all.'

Oh, God, he knew, he knew! she despaired. 'Y-you weren't the only one on board,' she still had to try and evade in an uneven murmur.

Glancing at her downbent head, Hunt expelled a heavy breath and with a hunching of wide shoulders began descending the steps himself. 'Okay. Then I guess there's nothing more to be said.'

Now Devon did look up, to gaze after him in bewilderment as he headed across the lawn towards the helicopter. He'd as good as said he knew she was in love with him, so why was he suddenly leaving? To show her he didn't care? But then he'd already admitted that's why he was there, hadn't he? In an agony of perplexity and indecision she began chewing at her lower lip.

'Well, Pauline said you were the new man in *her* life!' she called after him part accusingly, part reproachfully, and not a little distractedly.

'Did she really? That *was* nice . . . or nasty of her, wasn't it?' he half spun round in order to contend sardonically. 'It's a pity you didn't think to ask her if I'd ever given her any reason to believe she was the new girl in mine, though!' He continued walking.

'Well, wasn't she?' she both charged and cried at the same time.

This time he didn't even look back. He just shrugged, 'I told you the answer to that before. You didn't believe me then, so what's the point of my repeating it now?'

All of a sudden Devon's finely marked brows drew together in a frown. Could that be why he was leaving? Because, as he'd maintained previously, she did tend to unfairly put him on trial every time he opened his mouth? In a matter of seconds she was rushing across the grass after him.

'Hunt!' she shouted desperately on seeing him open the aircraft's door. 'Please . . . wait!'

To her relief he at least closed the door again, even if he didn't exactly turn to face her directly, but merely leant one shoulder negligently against the helicopter as he waited for her to reach him. Once she did, all her courage seemed to desert her and she flushed self-consciously under his unswerving gaze. Oh lord, she only hoped her thinking had been correct!

'Please d-don't leave,' she quavered. 'I really don't mean to make you—make you defend yourself all the time, you know, it's just that—it's just that. . .' She paused to swallow the constricting lump in her throat. 'I know I'm not as sophisticated and "with it" as all the other females of your acquaintance doubtlessly are, so I just had to protect myself somehow because I thought you'd—you'd probably only find me more amusing if I let you know how—how I really felt about you.' She gave a small, shuddering sob.

'Oh, Christ!' It was a groaned prayer Hunt uttered rather than an oath as he gathered her shaking form to him tightly. 'The only reason I tried to keep it light was because it was obvious, right from our very first meeting, just how delightfully innocent you really were, sweetheart! Certainly not because I was ever making fun of you,' he vowed huskily. 'Oh, true, I wasn't averse to having a shot at Wilkinson—it was just beyond me how he could treat you so indifferently when I would've given everything I owned to be able to possess you—but I can assure you none of them were ever intended for you, my love. Or, at least only in so far as to try and awaken you to the knowledge that there were far deeper emotions to be savoured than the dispassionate ones he'd evidently only demonstrated, and thereby hopefully steal you away from him.' His mouth lowered to her forehead. 'I've wanted you from the moment I first saw you in that lagoon, Devon, as naked as the day you were born, and so damned beautiful I couldn't take my eyes off you! I love you, little sea nymph, make no mistake about that!'

Devon tilted her head back, her eyes a radiant turquoise now as they lifted to his. 'Oh, Hunt, I love you too ... so much!' she owned fervently. 'I'm so thankful the cyclone brought you back.'

His arms tightened about her imperceptibly. 'I would have come anyway,' he revealed on a deep note. 'The thought of you perhaps going ahead and marrying Wilkinson nearly drove me crazy. I knew I had to have you, because I just couldn't come to terms with the idea of going through life without you. Cyclone Muriel simply precipitated my arrival.' He broke off, shaking his head despairingly in remembrance. 'Hell, I hope I never have to go through another night like the last! If anything had happened to you. . .'

'But nothing did,' she was able to smile happily. And with her slender arms sliding upwards to link lovingly around his neck and begin impelling his head down to hers, 'Although I am expecting more of this morning.'

Her message was plain, and so was the warmth of desire in Hunt's eyes as he willingly covered her lips with his in a kiss that shocked her with its depth of feeling and had her reciprocating more ardently than she ever had before.

'Oh, God, I want you more than I've ever wanted anything in my whole life!' he groaned unevenly against the softness of her mouth some long, electrically charged minutes later.

Devon's breath came raggedly. 'I want you too,' she breathed with simple eloquence.

Hunt shook his head in a distracted movement. 'Do you realise just what you're implying?' he queried on a thickened note.

She nodded, albeit a trifle shyly. 'I'm implying I love you without reservation, and—and that I want to be yours in the most complete way possible.'

'But you're so damned. . .'

'Inexperienced?' Her eyes lifted to his achingly. 'Then isn't it time that was rectified by the only man I've ever wanted to make love to me?' she smiled winsomely, and twined her arms even more tightly about the strong column of his neck when, with a muffled sound of helplessness, he swept her high against his chest and began striding towards the house.

Some considerable time later Devon roused herself sufficiently from her state of drowsy contentment to lift her head from where it had been resting against Hunt's bronzed and heavily muscled shoulder in order to gaze down at him adoringly. 'I love you, Hunter Kincaid,' she said throatily.

With a smile that had her heart turning over, he curved a hand around her nape and bent her head to his. 'No more than I do you, Devon Matthews,' he answered in deep-felt kind as he brushed his lips over hers lingeringly. 'You're all and more a man could ever wish for, and I want you as my wife as soon as it can possibly be arranged.'

As did she! Although in her new-born confidence that didn't stop her from bantering, 'I thought you said promises to marry weren't in your line.'

'Nor were they ... until a contrary, argumentative, but thoroughly captivating little sea nymph suddenly erupted into my life like summer lightning,' he grinned lazily. 'So perhaps you'd better listen carefully while I make my first and last such vow.' Propping himself up on his elbow, he held her gaze with loving eyes. 'Because I hereby promise to love, marry, cherish, honour and keep you for the rest of my life. Understand?' He smiled again.

'Enchantedly,' she sighed in blissful tones.

'And leaving the island?' he hazarded, his expression growing a trifle guarded. 'What are your feelings in that regard now?'

'You were the one who kept insisting it was the only thing I cared about,' she pointed out lightly. 'It meant a lot, I admit, but even so ...' she dimpled, 'it can't compete with what I'm getting in exchange.'

A statement for which she was rewarded extremely satisfactorily. 'And Wilkinson? Did you really only remove his ring because it was getting in the way?' Hunt then probed.

Devon shook her head. 'No, I took it off, as I think you suspected, because I knew I couldn't ever marry him feeling as I did about you.'

'So it's finally over between the two of you?' His pleasure at the thought was evident.

'Well, yes and no, actually,' she disclosed with a wry half laugh. 'It's over, yes, but unfortunately I haven't had an opportunity to tell Garth that as yet.'

'You'd better hurry and do so, then, or he's going to get one hell of a surprise to see someone else's ring on your finger, isn't he? That is, if he can bestir himself enough into paying you sufficient attention to even notice!' he added derisively. Then, in a return to his earlier indulgent tone, 'Because I mean to have that mark on your finger covered by a ring of mine, if not by the end of today, then by tomorrow at the latest.'

'So soon?' Devon gasped, although not without some appreciation. 'You really believe in moving fast once your mind's made up, don't you?'

'Uh-huh! And especially when you're involved,' he drawled. 'Besides, I want everyone to know you're very definitely spoken for.' His eyes crinkled engagingly. 'Because I know just what a temptation you can be.'

'One you didn't appear very taken with when you said I learnt too fast that night of the barbecue, though,' she reminded reproachfully.

'Didn't appear taken with!' Hunt repeated incredulously. 'Are you out of your mind? I was hard put not to just plain take you, there and then, I wanted you so much! By that time I was finding it damn nigh impossible to keep not only my eyes off you, but my hands as well!' He paused, his mouth sloping ruefully. 'Or hadn't you noticed?'

'I noticed it more, and missed it worse, once you stopped,' she confessed self-consciously. Then, with a diffident hunching of one shoulder, 'I thought you

just meant I was making it too easy for you, and that—
that you weren't very impressed.'

'You mean, *that's* why you apologised?' His eyes
held hers disbelievingly. 'I never did succeed in
working out why you had.'

She nodded.

'Oh, no! Never that, sweetheart!' His dismay was
genuine as he pulled her comfortingly closer again. 'As
I said, the opposite was more like it.'

'Then why did you ignore me so completely
afterwards?' She slanted an uncomprehending glance
upwards from under glossy lashes.

He exhaled wryly. 'Mainly, because your attitude
was anything but encouraging at the time, if you
recall. In fact, freezing would probably describe it
best. But also, I guess, because I *was* becoming tired
of having to defend my every word and action. I
figured I was wasting my time, and so spent the
remainder of my stay trying to convince myself I'd
had a lucky escape.'

'And did you succeed?'

'I thought I had until I realised you were crying
when we left, and then I knew I'd merely been
unknowingly waiting for just such a sign. Only by
then it was a little late to do anything about it
immediately. I still had to sign those papers with Matt
in Northport, and although I intended returning
straight afterwards, unfortunately no sooner had we
berthed than a message came through that necessitated
me going down to Brisbane. Then when I did manage
to return, and as worried as I've every been about
anything, I'm greeted with one of your snide remarks
as soon as I set foot to the ground.' He glowered at her
with mock ferocity.

'I'm sorry,' she apologised earnestly. 'It was just the only way I could think of to disguise my true feelings because I didn't think you reciprocated them. At least, not until you made that remark about it being pointless in repeating you'd never been interested in Pauline, which then set me thinking.' With a sigh, she buried her head against his smooth chest. 'Would you really have left if I hadn't explained how I felt?'

'I don't honestly know,' he answered thoughtfully. 'Although if I had, I doubt it would have been for long. Being unable to keep away from you appears to have become an integral part of my life,' with a delightfully dry smile. 'But at the same time, I reasoned there was still no guarantee you would admit how I suspected you felt if I told you I loved you first. Judging by the past, I wouldn't have been at all surprised if such a declaration didn't immediately prompt the accusation that I was only doing so in an effort to recoup some of the purchase price of the island.'

'Oh, no, I would never have thought of anything like that,' Devon protested laughingly. 'Well, I don't think I would have. Although I can understand how you could believe I might. However . . .' halting she eyed him mischievously, 'now that you have mentioned it, this does mean you'll be getting Cowrie considerably cheaper than you envisaged, doesn't it?'

'Uh-uh!' he grinned, shaking his head un-equivocally. 'Whatever you receive from the sale, beautiful, is yours! I want none of it! You're worth far more to me than mere money.'

Devon's lips found his unerringly. 'You do have a winning way with you, don't you?' she smiled, and then narrowed her glance expressively. 'When you're not being infuriatingly mocking and purposely aggravating, that is!'

Hunt gave a warm, utterly stirring laugh. 'When you rise to the bait so readily, my love, it's too great a temptation to forgo,' he grinned without the slightest show of remorse.

'I see,' she acknowledged, straight-faced, though her eyes gleamed. 'Then I shall just have to cultivate ways to defeat you, shan't I?' She began trailing her mouth slowly, sensuously, down his throat and across the firm flesh of his shoulder, while smoothing a hand exploringly over his broad chest.

With a convulsive shudder, Hunt moved so that he was leaning over her, his own mouth seeking hers, his hand cradling a rosy-peaked breast. 'You don't need any more than you have already,' he groaned deeply. 'I have the distinct feeling I'm the one who's going to need all the help I can get. You've even had me surrendering regarding Matt already.'

'How do you mean?' curiously.

He hunched a brown shoulder deprecatingly. 'Well, you seemed so worried about this proposed trip of his—even though I'm still inclined to think un-necessarily—that I decided to see if I could find a solution that would suit the pair of you.'

'And?'

'What's his equal love to sailing?' he countered drily.

'Fishing.' Her reply came without hesitation.

'Mmm, that's what I'd gathered,' he nodded. 'So I just casually put the suggestion to him that he might like to consider staying on here in charge of the game fishing boats we'll be providing for guests' use. No one knows the area better than he does, and I figured that since I was already employing one of my, hopefully, future in-laws, I may as well employ both of them.'

'And?' she queried again, but more urgently this time.

'He agreed,' Hunt said with a smile for her ensuing obvious delight and relief.

'Oh, thank you, thank you!' Devon threw her arms around him exuberantly. 'I love you for that more than you'll ever know!'

The curve of his shapely mouth grew teasing. 'I don't suppose I will . . . unless, of course you could think of some way which might just help to show me.'

'I do believe I know the very thing,' she sparkled, already moving against him invitingly, and very shortly proved to the unqualified satisfaction of them both that, indeed, she did.

# Take 4
# Exciting Books
# Absolutely
# FREE

Love, romance, intrigue... all are captured for you by Mills & Boon's top-selling authors. By becoming a regular reader of Mills & Boon's Romances you can enjoy 6 superb new titles every month plus a whole range of special benefits: your very own personal membership card, a free monthly newsletter packed with recipes, competitions, exclusive book offers and a monthly guide to the stars, plus extra bargain offers and big cash savings.

**AND an Introductory FREE GIFT for YOU.**
**Turn over the page for details.**

As a special introduction we will send you four exciting Mills & Boon Romances Free and without obligation when you complete and return this coupon.

At the same time we will reserve a subscription to Mills & Boon Reader Service for you. Every month, you will receive 6 of the very latest novels by leading Romantic Fiction authors, delivered direct to your door. You don't pay extra for delivery — postage and packing is always completely Free. There is no obligation or commitment — you can cancel your subscription at any time.

You have nothing to lose and a whole world of romance to gain.

Just fill in and post the coupon today to **MILLS & BOON READER SERVICE, FREEPOST, P.O. BOX 236, CROYDON, SURREY CR9 9EL.**

Please Note:- READERS IN SOUTH AFRICA write to Mills & Boon, Postbag X3010, Randburg 2125, S. Africa.

- - - - - - - - - - - - - - - - - - - - - - - - - - -

# FREE BOOKS CERTIFICATE

**To:** Mills & Boon Reader Service, FREEPOST, P.O. Box 236, Croydon, Surrey CR9 9EL.

Please send me, free and without obligation, four Mills & Boon Romances, and reserve a Reader Service Subscription for me. If I decide to subscribe I shall, from the beginning of the month following my free parcel of books, receive six new books each month for £6.60, post and packing free. If I decide not to subscribe, I shall write to you within 10 days The free books are mine to keep in any case. I understand that I may cancel my subscription at any time simply by writing to you. I am over 18 years of age.

Please write in BLOCK CAPITALS.

Signature _____

Name _____

Address _____

_____ Post code _____

## SEND NO MONEY — TAKE NO RISKS.

*Please don't forget to include your Postcode.*

Remember, postcodes speed delivery. Offer applies in UK only and is not valid to present subscribers. Mills & Boon reserve the right to exercise discretion in granting membership. If price changes are necessary you will be notified.

EP86

6R   *Offer expires December 31st 1984*